PRAISE FOR THE DENVER MOON SERIES

METAMORPHOSIS

"The skilled, perpetually poised detective shines brightly in this series, be it a novel, comic book, or any other format."

—**KIRKUS REVIEWS** (Starred Review)

THE MINDS OF MARS

"Recommended for all fans of speculative mysteries."

—**PUBLISHERS WEEKLY**

"*Denver Moon: The Minds of Mars* combines Blade Runner and the original Total Recall with a dash of old-school detective noir that is hard to put down and leaves the reader wanting more."

—**INDIEREADER**

"A searing mystery with a superlative, gun-toting protagonist."

—**KIRKUS REVIEWS** (Starred Review)

"This is cinematic science fiction, moving at a fast pace and building up a complex world."

—**CLARION REVIEWS**

"Readers looking for adrenaline-fueled and downright fun literary escapism should look no further than *Denver Moon.*"

—**BLUEINK REVIEW** (Starred Review)

"*Denver Moon: The Minds of Mars* is noir sci-fi at its best. A powerful story that is hard to put down and highly recommended for mystery and sci-fi fans alike."

—**MIDWEST BOOK REVIEW**

DENVER MOON

HEX PUBLISHERS

DENVER MOON

THE SAINT OF MARS

A NOVELLA

WARREN HAMMOND & JOSHUA VIOLA

This is a work of fiction. All characters, organizations, and events portrayed in this book are products of the authors imagination and/or are used fictitiously.

DENVER MOON: THE SAINT OF MARS

Copyedits by Jennifer Melzer, Aaron Lovett and Dean Wyant
Cover art by Aaron Lovett
Cover design by Aaron Lovett and Joshua Viola
Denver Moon logo by James Viola
Interior art by Aaron Lovett
Typesets and formatting by Ellen Hubenthal

A Hex Publishers Book

Published & Distributed by Hex Publishers, LLC
PO BOX 298
Erie, CO 80516

www.HexPublishers.com

Print ISBN-13: 978-1-7339177-0-4
Ebook ISBN-13: 978-1-7339177-1-1

First Hex Edition: 2019

10 9 8 7 6 5 4 3 2 1

Printed in the U.S.A.

For Grandpa (Bobby),
You'll never be forgotten.
-Josh

ACKNOWLEDGMENTS

THIS BOOK EXISTS BECAUSE OF THE HELP AND support of Mario Acevedo, Dustin Carpenter, Keith Ferrell, Angie Hodapp, Matt Hubel, Ellen Hubenthal, Aaron Lovett, Jennifer Melzer, Matt Van Scoyk, Dean Wyant and you, the reader.

Thank you,

Josh and Warren

CHAPTER ONE

I KEPT TO THE SHADOWS, BACK PRESSED AGAINST the wall, my head swiveling left and right. Scanning. Searching.

Two months of work and I finally had a name: Lucas Robbins. Age 47. Earthborn. Immigrated to Mars six years back. Address unknown.

The market was busy this time of day. Shift changes up and down the levs crowded the tunnels of this ant colony of a city. Hawkers pitched their wares. Amplified by scratchy speakers, their garbled voices drilled into my ears. Cooks worked fryers and griddles inside cramped booths soaked in bright neon. Electric fans lured customers by blowing the enticing odors of spiced faux meat out into the thoroughfares.

The latest missing person was last seen at the noodle bar down the way. That was two days ago. Two days since anybody had seen Millie Lopez, her last known meal a tofu bowl split between her and her mother, the noodle bar's prep cook.

A teenaged boy peeled off from the mass of people moving past. Approaching me, he touched a finger to the artery in his neck. I waved him away. Standing in the recesses like I was, he couldn't be the only one to mistake me for a quick-jab dealer.

<See anything, Smith?> I subvocalized to the AI installed in my gun.

<Facial rec still reporting no hits,> he said. <But I can't see very well from here. Even looking through your eyes, I can only make out about half of the faces well enough for comparisons. Any way you can get me to a higher location?>

I pulled the Smith & Wesson off my belt and reached up to balance him atop a drain pipe that ran the length of the wall.

<Turn me a little to the left, Denver, and move me closer to the edge.>

I complied, doing my best to give his visual sensors the broadest possible view while keeping the gun balanced on the rounded surface. <How's that?>

<Much better. Still can't see everybody, but I can see most as they pass.>

I arched my back and pressed my shoulders against the grimy wall. You'd think a sealed environment like the tunnels this far down would be spotless, but the dust from the terraforming project was an insidious bastard.

Try as we might to keep the whirling clouds of dust out, a fine, powdery grit still wormed its way through the filters, and along the corridors, and down the lifts and dropshafts, the stairwells and ladder tubes, to cover everything with a film I was told was red. I wouldn't know. All grit and grime is the same color to me, just like the people—the clothes they wear, the blood they spill. Other people see colors and shades. I just see Mars.

A headache started shoving at the backs of my eyes. I pushed harder against the rock wall. The kink between my shoulder blades didn't appreciate the pressure, but I pressed harder.

I needed a massage.

A three-day drunk or a four-day zone.

A month of sleep.

I needed another line of work, one that didn't have me tied up in knots and working around the clock. I needed a change of scenery, something other than endless corridors, featureless except for the conduits and pipes that carried power and water in, shit and piss out.

It started to rain.

That was what people called it anyway. I knew better.

It was recycled wastewater. Reclaimed piss from the people who lived in the surface domes above our heads. Their piss wasn't any purer than ours, not before it was 'cycled anyway. And it didn't come down on *their* heads a couple of times a week in a futile attempt to rinse the grit from the walls and floors. They got real rain, or what passed for it on Mars—fresh water showers straight from the ice-claimers. Sweet and clear and unused for millions of years. Once their streets were clean and their gardens watered, it ran into the sewer tubes and through the 'cyclers before being piped down to us so we could pretend it was raining.

Mist filled the stale air, dewy drops gathering on the ceiling and walls. I'd never seen real rain, but I knew this wasn't it. Reminded me of an old joke Smith pulled from my grandfather's memories he was patterned after: <Don't piss on my boots and tell me it's raining.>

But that's just what the topsiders did, and up there in the clean air under the domes they told themselves they were doing us a favor, letting their wastewater trickle down on all us unfortunates in the corridors and caverns beneath them. Their kind had a history of trickling down, a history that went all the way back to Earth long before anybody left it.

I rubbed the back of a hand against my eyes, wiping the water away.

<I got him,> Smith said.

I stood straight. Every nerve in my body began to tingle. For two months, I'd been working this dead end of a case. No evidence. No witnesses. No leads. Nothing at all until an hour ago.

I grabbed hold of Smith and thumbed off his safety. Taking a deep, wet breath, I stepped out of the shadows.

<Turn left,> whispered Smith.

The mist came down harder, and I blinked against it as I stepped into the crowd.

<He's twenty feet ahead, Denver.>

I moved deeper into the promenade, the noodle bar to my right. I glanced through the window. The security cams hadn't shown anything out of the ordinary when Millie Lopez walked out the door for the last time, but a half hour earlier the feeds showed a man slurping noodles by himself. A hat and glasses hid much of his face, but Smith had more than enough to work with when he cross-checked the restaurant's clientele against all the other security feeds of the last-known locations of each of the nine people who had gone missing since I was hired.

Finally, we had a match. Lucas Robbins. He'd been spotted walking past the pharmapit our third missing person liked to frequent. No sign of Robbins at any of the other locations we'd catalogued, but these hits were enough to know he was our guy. Seeing as both the pharmapit and the noodle bar were in this same market area, I hoped he might pass through frequently, and now, just an hour later, I was on his tail. That was how cases went sometimes. Nothing for weeks or months at a time, then it came all at once.

I picked up my pace, closing the gap between me and him, my gun held low, where nobody would notice unless they were looking for it. <That him in the brown coat?>

<That's him.>

My finger quivered on the trigger, eager to drop him. But that was a sloppy strategy. The smart play was to call the ministry of police and let them take it from here. But my client insisted on keeping the cops out. Not an unusual request down here in the lower levs. In fact, I didn't even know who my client was. Requesting anonymity was also pretty damn common down in the bowels, and anonymity was a service I was happy to provide as long as they paid well, and on time.

I moved closer so that there were only a few feet between us. A quick pulse was all it would take to collapse him into a twitching heap. But there were nine people missing. I figured them all for dead, but as long as there was a chance any were still breathing, I needed to follow him.

The space seemed to narrow as we snaked through a group of Church of Mars monks proselytizing and begging for alms. The crowd tightened around me, and despite my best efforts, I fell behind, my eyes squinting through the mist, struggling to stay locked onto his tall, angular frame.

I shouldered my way through a knot of people just in time to see him leave the main promenade and enter an alley, the falling water making him blurry to my eyes.

Quickening my pace, I tightened my fingers around Smith's grip as I entered the alley. Jammed full of stalls and food stands, the alley only afforded a single-file path. Yet he was gone. No sign of my quarry.

<Dammit, where did he go?>

<I don't know.>

I marched up to the first food stand where soyakebabs sizzled on a flat grill, their sputtering and popping echoed by droplets dribbling down from the alley's roof.

The little man tending the grill grinned, but before he could launch into his sales pitch, I pointed my gun at his face. The guy's eyes grew wide, and he swayed like he was about to pass out.

<Show him,> I subvocalized.

From the top of the gun, Smith projected a small hologram of Lucas Robbins.

"You see this man?" I asked, my voice sounding rough and harsh. It'd been some time since I'd spoken out loud. "You see where he went?"

The guy shook his head and spread his arms wide, the oily spatula in his right hand dripping with grease. "No. I didn't see anybody. I was—"

"Don't give me that. He just walked past two seconds ago."

"Lots of people do. I was flipping my kebabs."

I turned away and blocked the path of a woman headed for the promenade. I held Smith out so she could see the holo shimmering in the falling mist. "You seen him?"

The woman shook her head, and I moved on.

The alley was a dead end. There were only so many places he could have gone, and I worked them as quickly as I could, but none of the vendors or their customers would admit to seeing him. I was nearly at the end of the short tunnel before I had any luck—a small voice saying, "I saw him."

I looked down.

A beggar girl wrapped in a dirty blanket sat with an alms-bowl on a filthy scrap of rug. She spoke again, her voice a little louder this time. "I saw him come right by here but he didn't pop me any credits or even slow down when I asked."

Her face was streaked and smeared from the mist and dust. Her eyes were large and dark. The combination ought to have been good for business, but there was nothing in her bowl.

"Where did he go?"

"Won't say—not unless I get paid."

I bit off a curse, dug deep into my jacket pocket and flipped her a handful of credits, some of which missed her bowl.

She gathered the credits, but even as she did, she nodded at the facade of the metalworks shop that capped the end of the alley. "He went in there," she said.

"There any other ways in or out?"

"Nope," she said, her attention still on the credits now gathered in the bowl.

I was about to thank her, but something held me back. Something was off. I kept my eye on her as I stepped toward the door of the metalworks shop.

I gripped my gun tight in my fist. <You ready, Smith?>

<I was initialized ready.> Another one of his bad jokes.

Reluctant to take my eyes off of the girl, I jerked open the door and was flooded with bright light and flashing beams of what I assumed were different hues, but it all just looked like light to my colorblind eyes. I checked on the girl again. She sat right where I left her, and I held my breath for a second before I went inside.

I looked for the proprietor or an attendant, but there was no one. A digital voice sounded from a speaker near the door. “Welcome. How can I help you?”

<Roboshop,> Smith said. <Odd.>

It was—who would finance a totally automated shop at the end of a third-class marketplace on a lower level? I filed that question away for later, and ignoring the house AI’s repeating welcomes, I made a quick inspection of the place. Sparks showered from articulated welding lasers moving fast like spider legs. Near the door, boxes of cogs and circuit boards sat on shelves ready for pickup. Annealing guns and smelting pods blasted white-hot heat that made my damp clothes tighten around me.

<You sense any humans?> I asked Smith.

<Scans say not a one.>

I sighed heavily and ran my eyes around the shop one more time, my gaze coming to a section of bricks set into the wall. <You see that?>

<See what?>

I stepped up to the wall. <See how the mortar doesn't match?>

<No. Let me patch in to your eyes.>

I ran my fingertips over the mortar.

<I see it now,> said Smith. <Too much light pollution for me to see it with my own sensors.>

It didn't happen often, but every once in a while, my monochrome vision picked up something others couldn't see. Tracing the irregular trail of mortar with my fingers, I followed the line all the way down to the floor, where the lowest brick gave slightly beneath my touch. I pushed harder and the wall shifted, sliding aside to reveal a narrow, dark corridor cut through stone.

That sneaky bastard.

<Make yourself a little more intimidating,> I told Smith.

<Cannon mode?>

<No. Just a holo for now, we don't know what we're going to find. But make it a *scary* holo.>

Smith glowed for an instant and the gun's sleek lines disappeared beneath a hologram overlay that doubled its size and sprouted big over/under barrels and a balloon magazine.

<Bigger,> I said.

Smith shimmered again and blossomed into a triple-barreled weapon, belt-fed, with alternating explosive and penetration cartridges. He projected a long bandolier of ammo that stretched up to drape over my shoulders.

<Happy now?> Smith asked with a touch of impatience.

<Nice,> I said. <Let's go.>

I was four steps into the tunnel when I heard the wall slide shut behind me. I didn't look back. Smith bloomed a lightstalk and the tunnel ahead glowed softly. I took three more steps and heard the wall behind me slide open again.

I looked over my shoulder to see the beggar girl, her features cold and angry now. In a flash, I knew what bothered me about her. Her alms bowl had no rainwater in it. She must have just arrived in the alley when she claimed to see Robbins.

I barely started to dive for cover when she pulled the trigger of the gun she held in her hand.

Her gun was smaller than Smith, even without the holo projections, but it was big enough to fill the tunnel with nova-bright light that struck me hard and left me unconscious on the floor.

CHAPTER TWO

I WAS SO COLD. MY TEETH CHATTERED uncontrollably and my shoulders quaked. My vision was blurred and my thoughts weren't any clearer. The pain between my shoulder blades had turned into an unrelenting agony, like it was about to pull me apart. I closed my eyes and drew a deep breath of stale air thick with the smell of copper. I held it long enough for my vision to begin to sharpen.

My hands were tied together, tight, and the cord that bound my wrists was looped over a metal hook that might've been fabricated in the robotic metalshop that fronted this place, whatever this place was.

Other bodies hung from identical hooks, but none of their hands—those that still had them—were tied. Instead, their arms hung limp and lifeless by their sides. Some of the corpses had been decapitated, neck stumps protruding from sagging shoulders. Others still had their heads, but the tops of their skulls had been removed like lids from jars. Hoisted and impaled, their chests were pierced by sharp points. I held my breath again and looked down.

My feet dangled maybe twenty inches off the ground. The floor was dark with splotches and stains of blood. Long gutters carved into the stone ran to a large floor drain.

<For exsanguination,> Smith said.

Smith lay on a low metal table in front of me. A man's body lay beside him. <Exsangui— what?>

<Exsanguination. Bleeding out. You see the shunts inserted into the arteries in their thighs and wrists? They're used to let the blood drain out.>

<Great.>

<I've been trying to call for help, but this place must be shielded. I can't get any kind of signal. You need to find a way out of here, Denver.>

<No shit.> I tried to flex my fingers but I couldn't feel them. <I'm freezing. How long have I been hanging here?>

<Two hours and—>

<Long enough,> I said. <How many bodies can you see?>

<Dozens.>

Dozens? I shouldn't have been surprised the number was so much larger than the nine I knew of. The lower levs were crammed with lost souls who would never be missed.

Shivers shook my spine and rattled my teeth. It was

damn cold in here. I lifted my legs, then dropped them back down to get a small swing started. Screaming shoulders told me to stop, but I swung again, creating a wider arc. If I built up enough momentum, maybe I could get the cord linking my wrists off the hook.

A door slid open and the beggar girl came through. The blanket she had wrapped around her shoulders in the alley was gone. She wore a brown jacket so loose I realized it had been fitted for a grown man. Same for the pant legs that bunched around her ankles. She studied me for a moment, her large eyes moving slowly back and forth with the rhythm of my body. She shook her head and approached.

I prepared to kick her as hard as I could but she kept out of range and came in from behind before grabbing my legs. Her powerful grip dug painfully into the backs of my thighs, and she brought my swings to a stop. "Don't try that again," she said. Her voice was strong, no sign of the waif she'd played in the marketplace.

She stepped to the table where Smith lay beside the corpse. For a moment she didn't move, but then her eyes closed and she shivered gently before seeming to grow taller. I blinked to shake away what must have been a hallucination, but she continued to grow. The baggy-fitting brown jacket began to fill out, and under the fabric of the sleeves I saw arms stretching until fingers and hands emerged from the cuffs. Her face became more masculine, soft cheekbones hardening while her brow bulged to cut a sharp line over her eyes.

"Robbins," I said, my voice a hoarse croak.

<He's an alien,> Smith said into my head.

I knew the bugs could take human form, but shape-shifting in a matter of seconds was a trick that filled my stomach with dread. How could we stop them when they could transform their appearance at will? Maybe my grandfather was right. We couldn't hope to defeat them. One way or the other, we were destined to be their slaves.

The shapeshifter strapped the corpse's head to the table with metal bands, and arranged an array of tools and implements on the table's surface. When it was satisfied, it looked back at me, its eyes bright.

"I have a bit of work to do here," it said, "and thought you might appreciate seeing the process before it's applied to you. Actually, in your case, it might be necessary to perform my duties upon a *living* specimen."

"Lucky m-me," I said, shivering so bad it was a struggle to get the words out. "What is this p-place?"

The shapeshifter looked at my gun, its good fortune that the barrel was pointing the other way. "An Earth shooter, yes? Smith & Wesson, I believe, referred to in antiquity as a six-shooter. Of course, yours isn't entirely antique, is it? The holographic projection you installed was most impressive."

<It'll be more impressed if you can get a shot at it, Smith.>

<Believe me, Denver, I will as soon as I get the opportunity. As long as it doesn't know about me, we have a chance.>

"So w-what is this place?" I asked again, speaking as loud and tough as I could manage hanging from a hook with my hands numb and tied above my head. "You work for D-doctor Werner?"

The shapeshifter's attention turned on me, and Smith rotated his cylinder by one. In the process, his barrel turned a few degrees in the right direction. A half dozen more cylinder rotations and he might have a shot.

"You know my associate is g-going to come looking for m-me," I lied while Smith made another rotation, the click covered by my voice. "He knows w-where I am."

"Excellent. I have an empty hook with his name on it."

Smith rotated again.

"You won't be able to run your s-sick experiments on him. H-he's an android."

Another rotation.

"Their skulls open just as easy," the shapeshifter said as it lifted a circular saw and brought the device to life with a high-pitched whine. The shapeshifter bent over the corpse's head. The room filled with the thrum of metal cutting through flesh and bone. Loud enough to cover Smith putting the cylinder through two more rotations before the shapeshifter shut off the saw and stepped back to survey its work.

As long as it was looking at the skull, I let my eyes

flick back and forth between it and Smith, measuring the angle of the gun barrel and calculating the odds.

<Two more. Two more and take the shot.>

The shapeshifter peeled the top of the corpse's skull back and cracked it free.

It aimed a sick grin at me. "I wonder what the inside of your head looks like."

Smith moved partway through another cylinder click, but stopped when the shapeshifter glanced in his direction. The alien's eyes pinched a bit when it must have noticed that the gun's aim had turned. I held my breath, hoping it'd assume the table vibrations caused by the sawing made the gun move.

The shapeshifter tossed the skullcap toward a garbage can and it struck the wall with a wet slap before falling into the pail.

<I'm so close,> said Smith. <Almost there.>

<On three,> I said. I counted the digits for him, then screamed as loud as I could.

Startled, the shapeshifter jumped back and turned to me as Smith put himself through two more quick rotations.

The shapeshifter took a step toward me before—

Smith took a shot.

Best he could under the circumstances, but not good enough. The pulse sailed wide and shredded two of the hanging corpses, leaving tattered body parts swinging wildly from their hooks. Meanwhile, the kickback from the discharge sent Smith skittering along the table, his cylinder spinning as he tried to line his barrel up for another shot.

The alien lunged for the table. Smith fired again. Another miss, but this one was close enough to drive the 'shifter back toward me just as I bent at the waist and lifted my legs high and wide. I brought them down over the shapeshifter's shoulders, hooking my knees under its arms, my thighs locked tight around its neck as I furiously levered us both backwards.

The shapeshifter's added weight made my arms feel like they were about to pull from their sockets. Gathering its feet underneath, it raised its arms and slipped free of my hold. Swinging forward now, I summoned all the strength I had to yank on my restraints, lifting myself high enough that my head bumped the metal hook. Waiting for my oscillation to hit its apex, I jumped the cord off the hook. Airborne, I collided with one of the hanging corpses before tumbling hard to the floor.

The shapeshifter rushed the table again, giving Smith just enough time to fire. The pulse plowed through another corpse before the table toppled, dissection tools scattering across the floor. I got to my feet and staggered after the alien, but I was too slow. The shapeshifter grabbed Smith and pointed the barrel at my head.

"W-wrong move," I said through chattering teeth.

The instant those words left my mouth, Smith let loose an electric charge strong enough to spin the shapeshifter around and drop it screaming and twitching to the floor. The gun fell from its spasming grip and skittered toward me.

I picked up Smith with both of my bound hands, barely able to feel his familiar weight in my numb fingers.

<Cut me loose,> I said, breathing hard.

Smith extruded a small blade and sliced through the cords that bound my wrists. I moved him to my left hand and flexed the fingers of my right, my fingertips burning with the return of circulation.

I took a step toward the shapeshifter, who was still twitching. I knelt and put Smith's muzzle against its temple.

The shapeshifter trembled and became the beggar girl once more, staring up at me with the imploring eyes of a child who'd done wrong.

"Don't move," I said. My mind scrambled to decide on my next course of action. I wanted to question it for a long, painful time, but I couldn't be sure there weren't more of them down here somewhere. I thought about turning it over to the authorities, but it was an alien, and aliens were a secret. If word got out that they existed and were running our terraforming project, the delicate balance that kept this world inching toward a viable future would be destroyed.

The shapeshifter made up my mind for me when it grabbed a scalpel from the floor. I squeezed Smith's trigger and let him take off the top of the alien's head.

Smith was neither as neat nor as precise as the shapeshifter had been with his saw, but he got the job done. Bits of bone and brain, or whatever the bugs called it, splattered across the room. Black goo blew back to spray my hands and arms.

The alien shifted once again. Flesh and muscle melted into chitinous legs and arms. A sectioned body showed through its shirt. Its neck, long and narrow, led to a mantis-like head, what was left of it.

<Nice shooting,> Smith said as I raised his muzzle toward my mouth. He projected a holo of gun smoke and I pursed my lips to blow it away.

I stood and stretched my tingling arms. Again, I looked around this horror show of a space, and seeing so many people hanging like slabs of meat, any urge to celebrate quickly faded.

The alien didn't move. I figured it for dead, but I'd once seen one of them recover from a broken spine, so who was to say blowing their brains out counted as a kill shot?

<Denver?>

<What, Smith?>

<You see the top of the spinal column?>

I bent down to look inside the cranial cavity. <I guess so.>

<I just scanned it. Same for the chunk of brain that's still there.>

<And?>

<I think it’s human.>

CHAPTER THREE

I STARED AT THE CORPSE. OR WAS THAT WORD reserved for humans?

Should I call it a carcass? Carrion? Bug splat?

Disgusted as I was, Smith said the brain inside that chitinous skull was human. What were those alien bastards up to now?

My head throbbed, and the numbness in my arms and shoulders gave way to a grinding pain. Clenched teeth made my jaw ache. How had they managed to transplant a brain—an actual brain from an actual person—into one of their heads? And why?

<Denver, don't you think you should get out of here?>

Yes, I should. And never come back. Decapitations. Bodies hanging like sides of beef. An alien with a human brain. Jesus.

<Denver? There might be more aliens nearby. We need to go.>

I put one foot in front of the other but didn't head for the door. Instead, I navigated into the forest of swaying bodies on hooks. Not one still had its brain. The aliens were obsessed with the human mind. For twenty years, they'd been trying to turn us into drones. Worker ants for their interplanetary hive.

But they hadn't cracked the code. Not yet, anyway.

I recognized one of the corpses. It was Millie Lopez, the most recent to go missing. She was thirty-two years old, about the same age as me. Empty eyes stared from her abbreviated forehead, the top of her skull missing along with most of her hair.

Next to Millie was Keisuke Uchida. The wife of the man I'd visited two months ago when I first got started on this case.

<Denver, we have to go.>

I heard the words but they barely registered.

<Don't be such a stubborn little girl,> he said. Smith was pulling out the heavy artillery now, using the same wording my grandfather often used when I was young.

I looked down at him still clutched in my right fist. His silver plating was splattered with tacky black goo. I tucked him into my belt and peeled my skin away from the handle. <No. This woman has a family. They all have families. We can't leave them here to rot.>

<What if more aliens show up? What if somebody heard the commotion and comes in to check it out? The aliens are a secret.>

That they were. Some suspected, but very few knew the shapeshifters walked among us. How many there were, I didn't know, but I knew their leader was Dr. Stewart Werner, the same Doctor Werner who was turning our red planet green.

I wished I could just call the ministry and let them clean up this mess, but they couldn't be trusted to keep the bugs a secret. If their existence ever leaked to the general public, Mars City would be overrun by lynch mobs. As much as I wanted to lead the charge myself, the truth was, we needed them. Without their technological knowhow, the planet would never be terraformed, and if Mars couldn't sustain humanity for the long term, we were doomed to extinction.

That was the impossibly fine line humanity had to walk. The razor's edge upon which those of us who knew the secret were balanced. On the one hand, we couldn't survive without a viable new home after we'd pretty well destroyed our old one. On the other hand, we couldn't become mindless slaves like so many other races conquered by the bugs.

So, we hid their true intentions and hoped that against all odds, our minds proved impossible to crack.

<Denver?>

<Call Hennessey as soon as you have a signal again. Tell him what happened here.>

<You're joking. You hate that man.>

I did. The Peerless Leader of the Church of Mars was

a snake, but he was on humanity's side. He was the only one on this planet fighting against their mind control. There hadn't been many cases of red fever since I crashed the Minds of Mars into the surface of this shithole six months ago—something I couldn't have done if it hadn't been for Hennessey. He did his best to teach meditation and a stringent form of self-discipline to that cult of his. I had no idea if his techniques were actually capable of shielding our minds from the alien attacks, but at least he was trying.

That was more than I could say for my grandfather. Tatsuo Moon and Hennessey were once the best of friends, co-founders of Mars. Until the aliens arrived. The shapeshifters infiltrated our population and then when they were firmly entrenched, Doctor Werner revealed himself to offer them a deal.

Of course, the deal was no deal at all. Sure, he offered to terraform Mars, but the price was the complete enslavement of the human race. Only a select few would remain free of mind control. Only that select few would be offered powerful positions in the governorship of Mars.

Hennessey said no. My grandfather said yes. He and I would be spared.

I stood before a male corpse. He'd been hanging here long enough to gather a film of gritty dust and an odor as foul as the deepest bowels of the methane pits. Tattooed on his forearm was a baby's face with a date of birth written underneath. His son was only four years old. I looked up to find the man's face, but only found an empty space above his shoulders.

His mind had been taken, stripping him of everything he ever was. Of every memory of the child branded on his arm. Stripping his son of a father. This man meant nothing to the bugs. Just another lab rat on a planet full of lab rats. How could my grandfather make a deal with those monsters? How could he betray his own people?

Hennessey recently told me he'd said those exact words to my grandfather. Still, Ojiisan wanted to make the deal. That was when Hennessey kidnapped him, wiped his memory, and exiled him to live the rest of his years alone in the southern deserts.

I didn't know any of that history when I rescued him. I didn't know about any deal when I gave him his memories back. I was the one who put humanity at greater risk by making it possible for him to reestablish his godforsaken deal.

<Denver?>

<Did you send a message to Hennessey?>

<We still don't have a signal.> He sighed just like my grandfather. <Don't you want to think about it? You know Hennessey tried to kill you.>

"I told you to send the message!"

I spun on my heel only to find another corpse. I pushed past it, and past another and another until I found open space. My hands were clenched into fists, my lungs heaving in and out. It was rare that I spoke aloud to Smith, but damn, he really pushed my buttons sometimes. I knew it wasn't his fault, but as the carrier of Ojiisan's memories for so many years, he'd taken on much of his personality. Thankfully not the bad parts like being a traitor to humanity, but even if Smith represented the best of my grandfather, there were times when the very thought of my Ojiisan—the traitor who lovingly raised me—sent me into a rage.

Hennessey had indeed tried to kill me, and he'd done it more than once, but who else could I call? He would know how to clean up this mess. That church of his was a secret society inside of a secret society. He had priests who knew how to keep their mouths shut. They'd dispose of the alien and find a way to get the bodies back to their loved ones.

All that mattered was preserving the status quo. Much as it made me want to vomit, the balance between us and the aliens had to be maintained. What other chance did we have?

I headed out the door back to the metalworks shop. I had to get home. Had to get cleaned up. I had to learn more about Lucas Robbins and this laboratory of his. Whatever these experiments were about, they had to stop.

The aliens couldn't win.

<Signal established. The message has been transmitted.>

I shook my fists loose and let out a deep sigh. <Good. Thank you, Smith.>

CHAPTER FOUR

I DROPPED MY DIRTY SHIRT INTO THE GARMENT cleanser along with the rest of my clothes. Crossing my one-room apartment, I stepped behind the glass door where a showerhead hung from the ceiling. Lukewarm water drizzled onto my head and I soaped my hands, inky swirls of bug gunk spiraling down the floor drain.

I leaned against the rock wall, the roughly carved surface feeling cool against my back. I let out a long breath, and my muscles finally started to unknot.

<You have three messages.>

<Jesus, will you let me relax for a minute?>

Closing my eyes, I let water rain on my face. I lifted my hands for my hair, but only made it halfway before my shoulders locked in pain.

<Should I make a doctor appointment?>

I opened my eyes to glare through the glass at the gun sitting on my table.

<Sorry,> he said. <Get back to relaxing.>

Again, I closed my eyes and tried to clear my head, but for months now I'd been powerless to close the flood-gates against the waves crashing through my mind. Fears big and small. The continuous rehashing of recent events always leading me to this same hellish spot, drenched by the shame my grandfather brought upon me, the weight of the world threatening to push me underwater.

Gods, what if I hadn't managed to get off that meat hook? What if Smith wasn't there to help? What if Robbins had realized the gun had an AI installed inside?

He would've cut my skull open. He would've pulled my brain out and put it inside one of *them*. Would I still be conscious of where I was? Would I still be me? Would I be screaming like a lunatic trapped inside a cage?

My heart was pounding now, my lungs working double time. I wished I knew a way to stop these kinds of thoughts. The only thing that worked—barely—was getting zoned. But even then, the gears continued to grind just under the surface, chewing and clawing their way into my consciousness.

You'd think I'd get used to my new reality. It had been six months since I rescued my grandfather. Six months since I learned just how precarious a position all humans were in. By now, I should know how to deal with it. I shouldn't find myself missing entire conversations as if I'd fallen asleep. I shouldn't find myself lying awake every night. I shouldn't be trolling pharmapits looking for any kind of high that could, even for the briefest of time, shut my mind off.

A part of me died six months ago. I'd been honest with myself about that at the time, but by now, I thought the other parts of me would've picked up the slack.

Maybe there was something to be said for the Church of Mars' meditation techniques. I knew now they were designed to block out the horrors of alien mind control, but maybe they could block the horrors of my life too. Maybe I needed to trade my longcoat for a silk robe. Maybe I needed to shave my head and act like I had all the answers.

I turned off the water and dried myself off. <Ok, tell me about those messages now.>

<You have two from your grandfather. Want to know what he said?>

<No. Delete them.>

<He wants you to come to the anniversary dinner of Mars' founding. You know he's receiving special recognition.>

<I know. Delete them.>

<Done. Message number three is from Jard Calder. He says he wants to hire you.>

I supposed that was good timing since I'd just finished my last job. Other than notifying my anonymous client, the case was over. I supposed I needed to notify the worried families of the deceased I'd interviewed, too. Gods, that wasn't going to be easy. Lately,

I'd been preferring to let Smith handle communications with my clients. A matter of efficiency was my official rationale. The real reason was I couldn't trust myself to stay sober long enough to pull off a productive meeting, especially one as emotionally fraught as notifying next of kin.

Maybe this once, I'd try to meet my client in person. I'd been hired anonymously, but there were ways to track the money down. Whoever my client was, he or she deserved the respect of hearing from me in person. But that couldn't happen until after Hennessey finished his clean-up of the scene. I'd probably hear from him in a few hours, once he decided on a good cover story for the abominations that occurred in that lab. I didn't want to lie about what really happened, but I'd be able to tell my client the truth about the important things. *Your loved one was murdered. The killer is dead.*

I wouldn't stop investigating the bigger picture. The aliens were accelerating their experiments, and the fact that I'd destroyed their last disturbing source of lab specimens six months ago was likely the primary cause. Whatever they were up to now, I'd destroy that too. As long as our minds stayed secured, we had a chance.

<Smith, I want everything you can get on Lucas Robbins. Find out who owns that metalworks shop, and go back through the footage you recorded in that lab. See if you can ID the other bodies.> The struggle continued.

In the meantime, I had to pay the bills. <And call

Jard. Tell him I'm available right now if he still wants to hire me.>

CHAPTER FIVE

I TURNED OFF OF RED TUNNEL TO ENTER ONE OF Mars' many tight alleyways. Neon signs encroached from every direction, strangling the corridor down to a narrow path where botsies danced on podiums and poles. A short walk ahead was the door to Jard's Pleasure Pit.

But the door was blocked. A trio of monks sat on the ground, plasma chains looped around their necks and through the door handles. One of them, a man wearing a hooded robe, spotted me and raised a finger of accusation. "Sinner!"

"No more sex slaves!" shouted one of the two men.

"Preach to somebody else," I said. "I have business in there, real business."

"We're not moving."

"Does the church know you're doing this?"

"Of course," said the man, his features hidden in the shadow of his hood. His voice was deeply resonant, his posture perfect as a yogi. I bent low to get a better look at his face.

"The time for discussion has long passed," he said. "This is a time for action."

From behind, a hand landed on my shoulder. I spun to find one of the pole dancers, her hair was impossibly tall and threaded with strands of light. An animated serpent tattoo slithered across her athletic frame. "Come, Jard is waiting. I'll take you in through the back."

Circling back the way I'd come, she led me into a neighboring alleyway, then through a steel door in the wall of rough-edged rock. A long, narrow room stretched ahead. A bench ran the length, and the room's walls were lined by metal lockers. Botsies—men, women and combos—stood or sat in various states of undress. Tall mirrors propped between lockers stretched to the ceiling, each one occupied by one or two botsies customizing their hair and makeup, adjusting skin hues or checking their attire.

"Shift change," said the dancer. "This way."

I followed her past a row of showers and into the showroom. Plush furniture sat around the exterior. Male botsies stood in various poses, arms crossed over bare chests or leaning against the wall like brooding teens. Most of the women reclined on sofas or settees, their skirts hiked to daring heights.

I'd never stood behind the glass before, inside the fishbowl. Thanks to the barricaded entrance, there was only one john on the other side. He had a hand on his chin, his brow furrowed like he was a really discerning customer. His eyes met mine and a shiver ran up my spine knowing he must think I was part of the merchandise. The dancer ushered me through another door and up a set of stairs to Jard's office.

The office was a large one. Jard wasn't the kind of man to do anything small. The floor was covered by lush white fur that, thanks to some unseen tech, waved like grass in a windstorm. The walls were covered by faux pelts of long extinct Earth species including zebra and leopard and giraffe. Jard sat at his desk, his tall-backed chair seeming more like a throne. "Denver," he said, augmented neon eyes glowing like always. "Come. Take a seat."

I sat opposite his desk and sank into the ample cushioning.

"It's been a few months," he said. "You look even shittier than the last time I saw you."

I responded with a wry smile. "I don't doubt it. What's the job?"

"Right to the point, eh? You'll never change. Did you see those fools chained to my door on your way in?"

"The job, Jard. What's the job?"

"Keep your pants on, kid. Now did you see those damn CoMers or not?"

"I did."

"Those assholes are killing my business, Denver.

They're spewing all kinds of crazy, saying my botsies are slaves."

I raised an eyebrow. A year ago, I would've said that was ridiculous. Botsies weren't people. They were things. Sure, they had the uncanny ability to imitate a human, but they were still appliances, no more worthy of sympathy or empathy or any other kind of pathy than a refrigerator. But that was before I witnessed the tragic death of Ana. Before I met Nigel.

He flamed a cig-stick, and took a long draw. "Don't give me that look, Denver. I don't pretend to be a perfect person. I know my business isn't proper, but it is necessary. People have their vices. Try as they might, they can't legislate or pray those vices away." He blew out a cloud of smoke that smelled of vanilla and berries. "All the things a botsie can do, and you know what they were used for first? It wasn't running a jackhammer in the mines. Their oldest profession is the same as ours."

"I'm not judging," I said.

"Yes, you are. But I accept that. Lots of people judge me by what I do for a living, but I hope you've known me long enough to see that I care about my botsies. If these CoMers put me out of business, things will get a lot worse for them. If they don't get bought up to work endless shifts in the mines, it'll be some other pimp who takes title, and believe you me, it will probably be one of those anything-goes pricks who sell cutting and amputation and all kinds of sick shit. I might be a real bastard, but you know my botsies could do worse. A lot worse."

He snapped his cig-stick to his mouth and smoke puffed out his nose. "That's what makes me so damn angry. Of all the businesses that use botsies, they come after me? I pay my botsies. I give them regular off-hours. Hell, I give them vacation days now, and still the damn church comes after me? What gives?"

"You made your point," I said. "But aren't you blowing this out of proportion? A few monks chaining themselves to your door doesn't qualify as a crisis. You've got botsies stationed in bars and clubs all over Mars City. The church can't block all those doors."

He pulled the cig-stick from his lips and waved it angrily about as he spoke. "They're not just barricading doors. They're harassing my customers. They're taking pictures and publishing the photos. They're spreading rumors about some bullshit disease, as if you can catch a disease from a botsie. Last week they followed one of my customers home and beat the shit out of him. They put him in the clinic, Denver. He's not going to eat solids for months."

"Are they doing this to any other botsie parlors?"

"There are two others that I know about. Both of them decent places with good reputations." The cig-stick went back in his mouth, smoke curling before his glowing eyes.

"Maybe it's time to make a donation," I said with a smirk.

"That's real funny, Denver. I already threw enough credits their way to build a cathedral. The Peerless Leader isn't calling the shots on this one. It's Bishop Ranchard."

I cringed at that name. My shoulders tensed and my molars ground tight. Rafe Ranchard and I had a history, and it wasn't a good one.

Jard pointed his cig-stick at me. "Have you heard the things he's been saying? He calls botsies humanity's children. He says anybody who consorts with one is a pedophile." He slapped his desk. "A pedophile!"

"I've heard."

"Why the hell did the Peerless Leader reinstate that whackjob? How senile is that old codger? He not only welcomed Ranchard back but he made him a bishop, too? Ranchard was batshit before he got excommunicated, and he's only gotten crazier since. He's dangerous, Denver."

"Trust me, I know that better than anybody."

"I know you do," he said as he leaned forward, cig-stick pinched between his teeth. "You were the one who got him excommunicated in the first place, weren't you?"

"That was Hennessey who gave him the boot, but yes, I played a role. Rafe hasn't forgiven me."

"Well, he needs to get checked, and fast. Now that he's back in the church, you better believe he plans to succeed Hennessey to become the new leader. Hennessey's a tough old bastard so I don't doubt he's got quite a few years left, but I don't trust Ranchard to not make a move before then."

"Agreed," I said. "So, what do you want from me?"

"I want you to get him excommunicated again. You did it once, you can do it again."

Finally, I thought. After all these years as a PI, I'd finally landed a job I could really enjoy. I wasn't the type to hold a grudge, but in the case of Rafe Ranchard, I made an exception. He'd done me dirty a couple times recently, so taking him down a peg or three wasn't just a chance to get even. It was overdue.

I held back the smile pushing at the corners of my mouth. I didn't want to give anything away before we got to negotiating a price. Instead, I shook my head and went into downplay mode. "The last time I helped to get him excommunicated, I had access to church records. That was how I found out he was embezzling. So, sure, if the church hired me, I might find something incriminating. But you're not the church. Where would I even start?"

"Come now," he said. "You're more creative than that."

I held my hands out like I was helpless. "For all I know, he's cleaned up his act."

"Don't bullshit me, Denver. You know that man is corrupted to the core."

"Being a crazy-ass zealot isn't illegal."

"It doesn't have to be illegal. It just has to be enough to pressure Hennessey into kicking his ass back out. Let him try to mobilize his fanatics then. He's nothing without the church's backing. Hell, you could plant a dildo on him for all I care. I'll take anything that will show the church he isn't the reformed man he claims to be."

I nodded like I had to think it over. As if I'd turn down the chance to get some righteous payback. My fingers tingled with the thought of it. Okay, maybe I was the type to hold a grudge. But this might be exactly what I needed. Maybe a little vengeance would deliver me from this funk I'd been in.

Again, I fought the smile off of my face. "That's a risky job."

"Name your price," he said, his artificial eyes shining like radioactive crystals.

"I've never done a job like that. Underhanded isn't my style."

"Name your price, Denver."

"Like I said, I wouldn't even know where to start."

"Name it."

I leaned forward and met those bright, glowing eyes head-on. "Fine. My price is Nigel."

CHAPTER SIX

"NIGEL?" ASKED JARD. "WHAT ARE YOU TALKING about?"

"I do this job, and you give me ownership of Nigel."

"You want one of my botsies? He that good a lay?"

I rolled my eyes. "I'm not joking, Jard."

He licked his fingers, and with a sizzling pinch, he snuffed the cig-stick's fire. "You know how much a botsie is worth?"

"I do."

"The manufacturing costs are astronomical, and they're getting more expensive. There's only one company still building parts, and those parts are taxed like you wouldn't believe. The other factories have all been coopted by the government, all resources directed toward Project Jericho."

"I know. They need to accelerate the terraforming." The new push was Hennessey's doing. The last six months, he'd pulled every last string he could to get the government to take such drastic measures. The race was on. Even shaving a decade off the centuries-long project could be the difference between a thriving new home for humanity and having to succumb to our alien overlords.

"It's not just the manufacturing costs, Denver. You have to factor in all the revenue Nigel will earn in the future."

"What revenue? He hasn't earned you a penny in six months."

"You're the one who got him shot."

"Why haven't you fixed him up?"

"Have you been listening? Parts are hard to come by. His entire torso had to be sold for scrap."

"Don't tell me you can't afford a new one."

"It's on backorder. And now he needs new legs, too."

"Why? His legs weren't damaged."

"I can't just let a pair of legs go unused. Since the torso was on backorder, I went ahead and repurposed the legs."

"Well, purpose them back," I said. "I get Nigel or no deal."

Jard leaned back in his chair, his head shaking slow from side to side. "You really care about him that much?"

"He took that shot for me." I didn't go on to mention the fact that if I'd died, my grandfather would've delivered thousands of brains to the aliens. Without Nigel, the experiments they would've run on those brains might've already led to humanity's enslavement.

"What would you even do with him?"

"He told me he wants to work for me, and since his chip has been on ice the last six months, it's not like he's had the chance to change his mind."

"What would he do?"

"I need a bodyguard."

"That thing on your belt not doing the job?"

<My thought exactly. What gives?>

"Smith is a good friend," I said for the benefit of both he and Jard. "But lately I've been accumulating more enemies than friends. A little extra protection couldn't hurt. Maybe after a while, after Nigel learns the job, I can expand the business by having him do some investigations of his own."

"I can't do it," said Jard as he crossed his arms. "What would I tell the other botsies? If I let this one go, the others might think they have alternative career paths, too."

"You'll think of something," I said. "You just told me you cared about your botsies. They're not things to you. Nigel's served you well, hasn't he?"

"The English gentleman shtick he does scores top dollar," he said. "All the more reason I can't let him go."

"Easy enough to copy his speech patterns. You've done fine the last six months without him."

He stared at me for a long while, eyes giving nothing away.

"That's my price," I said.

Finally, he shook his head. “You really want this? Owning a botsie isn’t as easy as you think. There are repairs. Registration fees. There’s a dozen security services you have to re-up every year to keep him malware free.”

“I know.”

“No, you don’t, but who am I to argue? We have a deal. Get Rafe Ranchard off my ass, and you can have Nigel.”

“Plus expenses,” I said with a grin.

“Jesus, Denver. Yes, expenses too. Now are we done?”

I stayed where I was. “I need Nigel.”

“You need him now? Goddammit, Denver, I told you his torso is on backorder. You’ll get him when you finish the job.”

“I need him now. Did you know one of those monks chained to your door is a botsie? His hood hides it, but I stole a good look.”

He blew out a tired breath. “No, I didn’t know that.”

“You don’t sound surprised. You know Bishop Ranchard’s message appeals to the botsies. That’s a big part of why you called me in, isn’t it? You’re not just afraid of losing your customers. You’re also terrified you’re going to lose your employees.”

He gave me a sober stare. “So?”

“They say Rafe grants asylum to botsies who escape from the mines. He hides them somewhere deep inside one of the churches.”

“Where are you going with this?”

"Well, one of those botsies is sitting outside your door right now. Rafe isn't hiding them anymore. He's pressing them into service. If you ask me, what you have outside your door right now is a recruitment poster."

"And?"

"If we're going to penetrate Rafe's inner circle, I say we offer Rafe a new recruit."

CHAPTER SEVEN

I OPENED MY EYES AND ASKED SMITH FOR THE time.

<You slept a little longer than two hours.>

Not bad, I thought. Two consecutive hours of sleep was close to a record these days. <Any word from Jard?>

<He called ten minutes ago. Nigel's chip is installed, and he's ready for pickup. I thought it best to let you sleep a little longer.>

<Thanks.> I sat up, and tried to lift my arms. Stiff as hell. I guess I should count myself lucky my shoulders hadn't dislocated when I hung from that hook.

I stood, and even though I'd slept on top, I still straightened the satin sheets. I had to give Jard credit, this room was pretty nice considering it had an hourly rate. I rinsed my face in the sink and put my hair into a ponytail. <Any other updates?>

<I tracked down the owner of the metalworks shop.>

<Who is it?>

<Stanislaw Mining.>

<You're joking.>

<I'm not. The mine sells off its cheaper ores there. The shop specializes in custom parts. Upload your design, and they'll manufacture your cog or widget or whatever it is you need.>

I went out the door. Ignoring the moans I heard coming from several rooms, I headed for the stairs that led to Jard's workshop. <Does Stanislaw own the space in the back, too?>

<They do. Originally, that space was used for storage, but they downsized the shop a few years ago, and the extra space has been sitting empty ever since.>

I dropped down the steps. <Do you think Stanislaw management knew what was going on there?>

<Impossible to tell. As you saw, the metalworks were fully automated, so there was no staff present. Whoever set up that lab went out of their way to hide the entrance, so it's not unreasonable to think Stanislaw Corp knew nothing about it.>

I wasn't sure I agreed. Nobody on Mars trusted the corps, not after what they did to Earth. I pushed through double doors into a small workspace. Jard sat in the only chair, a soldering gun hovering over a vise clamping a detached foot.

"Don't you have techs to do this kind of work?" I asked.

"Yes, but I still enjoy it sometimes. That's how I started, you know."

"As a tech? Never would've guessed."

He smiled. "I was a good one too. I used to work for Madame Fernek. Know her?"

"Not personally, but I know who she is."

"Botsies weren't as advanced back then. Us techs had to be artists, you know. I worked for her for six years before I started out on my own." Smoke rose from the end of the soldering gun and Jard took a deep breath. "Nigel's chip is in. He's all yours."

"Excellent. You made the right choice, Jard."

He put the gun down, pulled an articulated light over, and leaned in to inspect his work. I waited where I was until he looked up at me.

"What are you still doing here?" he asked.

"I need Nigel."

"I told you to take him."

"Where is he?"

He blinked those glowing eyes. "On the shelf."

I looked to my left at a bookcase crammed with paints and epoxies, spools of wires and synth-skin. "Where?"

"Bloody hell, Denver, I'm right here." Propped up against a tool box was a head. Nigel's head.

"Goddammit, Jard, where's the rest of him?"

"I told you his torso is on backorder."

"What the hell am I supposed to do with a head?"

"You wanted him, you got him," said Jard. "Now as your new British botsie would say, piss off."

CHAPTER EIGHT

I EXITED JARD'S THE SAME WAY I CAME IN. THE alley was empty other than a pair of trash cans near the end. Neon light bled across the pavement while I held Nigel's head by the hair like some gladiator carrying her prize, wires hanging from his open neck like strands of gore.

I raised him up so we could talk face-to-face. I wanted to tell him he was mine now. No, not mine.... I might be taking title, but I wasn't his owner. I had so much to say but looking at his face as it ridiculously bobbed and dangled from my fingers, I couldn't speak.

Instead, a burst of laughter boiled up from someplace deep inside, and the stern mask I'd been wearing for so long finally cracked. Snorts erupted from my nose, and I reached for my spasming gut.

Nigel smiled as he wobbled wildly from my quaking hand. "Much obliged," he said.

Hearing the prim form of British gratitude coming from his decapitated head, I only laughed harder. Nigel waited patiently, maintaining that same smile as the hilarity that had a hold of me ran its course.

Wiping my eyes, I said, "Sorry it took me so long to get you out of there. I didn't have the credits."

"I've been iced the whole time. Went by in a blink."

"I suppose it did. My arm is getting tired. You're heavy. How the hell am I supposed to carry you around with me everywhere I go?"

He seemed to think it over for a few. "How about on a pike? That would inspire some shivers, wouldn't it?"

After an hour in the alley—me sitting on the ground, Nigel wedged up against the wall to keep him from rolling—I'd managed to catch him up on the two jobs we had to work. He had plenty of questions about them both, especially the alien lab, but it was the other case we were going to approach first. The excommunication of Rafe Ranchard.

"Let's get to it," Nigel said.

Nabbing a plastic bag from one of the trash cans, I stepped out of the alley, turned the corner, and marched up to the monks chained to Jard's door. The bag swung from my right hand, Nigel's head hanging heavy like a melon inside.

"You ready?" I asked.

Nigel mumbled confirmation from the bag.

I checked over my shoulder—twice—to sell the idea I was nervous before leaning down to talk to the hooded botsie I'd seen before.

"You work for Bishop Ranchard, don't you?"

"I work for the Lord," he said, his glowing eyes in shadow.

I bent lower and whispered so only he could hear. "Is it true you have a safe haven?"

His squinted eyes were visible now. "I have no idea what you're talking about."

Opening the bag, I let the botsie monk peek inside. "I freed him," I said. "Just took his head so I could smuggle him out with nobody noticing. He needs asylum."

Nigel acknowledged the botsie with a smile. I threw the bag over my shoulder, dropped a small note and turned away before he could respond. I heard him call from behind, but I didn't slow down. The note had the anonymous comm account of a ghost contact. With any luck, somebody from Rafe's order would come calling.

Hustling back into Red Tunnel, I ducked into a murder-sim house, lingering just inside the door and looking out the window to make sure nobody followed. Blood curdling screams sounded in the background. Then I heard gunfire. I kept my eyes looking out the window.

<Think it's going to work?> asked Smith.

<I have no idea. But Rafe has never met Nigel, so as

long as I don't show myself to him, he's got no reason to think he and I have a connection. Contact Jard and delay the transfer of Nigel's title as long as you can in case Rafe looks up his ownership record. If we're lucky, we'll bait Rafe or one of his underlings into offering asylum.>

<You really think you can get Rafe excommunicated?>

<I don't know,> I said. <But if I can get Nigel on the inside, we'll find out how many botsies he has and where he's keeping them. Knowing Rafe, I'm sure he's up to a lot more than harboring botsies.>

The screams and whimpers of simulated murders sounded from somewhere inside the kill zone behind me. I tuned them out and kept my eyes trained on the window. Still no sign of anybody following.

<I know you don't want my advice,> said Smith, <but I urge you to go back to Jard and tell him you changed your mind. Provoking a man like Rafe Ranchard is dangerous. A little payback isn't worth the risk to you or that chattering head you're carrying.>

<Chattering head? Feeling a little threatened, are we?>

<Threatened by a pentaquad processor? I don't think so. I just don't think you need to be fighting Jard's battles. Let that pimp save his own business.>

<Rafe damn near killed me, Smith. He kidnapped my grandfather. Every time I see him, that dementedly intense stare of his gives me the chills. He's the kind of bad you can't wash off.>

<You're letting your emotions color your decisions.>

<Damn straight I am. But I'm not just doing it for myself. All of Mars is going to thank me for taking out that trash. That's what's going to make this revenge so sweet, Smith.> A grin threatened to break across my face. <This is the rare kind of vengeance that serves a higher purpose. This is the pure kind, and it comes guilt free.>

Startled by the revving of a chainsaw somewhere behind me, I looked over my shoulder to find the murder-sim ticket agent, a gray-haired woman stationed behind a thick pane of glass. "You goin' in or what?" she asked.

Without responding, I pushed my way out the door, back into Red Tunnel. Not really having any place I needed to be, I moved with the crowd, Nigel's head lightly bumping my knee as he rode inside his bag. Poor guy couldn't see a thing in there. I was going to have to come up with a better way of carrying him until he received a new torso.

Surrounded by low-rent botsie parlors, I pushed toward the plaza where buskers juggled and feve-ravaged derelicts panhandled. The shouts of a protestor caught my attention. A handmade placard hung from a string looped around his neck, words written in an urgent scrawl. *YOUR BROTHER IS AN ALIEN! YOUR SISTER IS AN ALIEN! YOU ARE AN ALIEN!*

People gave him a wide berth like his kind of insane was contagious. If they only knew crazies like him weren't crazy at all. He'd probably seen one of the shapeshifters in their natural form. Or maybe he saw one morph from one form to another. Whatever he saw, it would never be acknowledged. The secret had to be kept.

I passed close so I could drop a few credits into the paper cup at his feet. <Smith, have you heard from Hennessey?>

<Not yet.>

I started up some steps. One lev up was a food market, and I knew a stall in the back that offered decent bento boxes. <Ring him so I can have a little chat.>

<Why?>

<Much as I'm dreading it, I need to call my client and tell whoever it is what happened to the victims, but I can't do that until I know Hennessey has the scene wrapped. Plus, I need to know what kind of cover story he invented so I don't trip all over myself when the client starts asking questions.>

<I just scanned the news wires. Nothing's gone public yet, nothing about those people or what happened to them.>

<Call Hennessey anyway.>

<Why?>

<Dammit, Smith, what's your problem?>

<There's no problem, Denver. I'm just trying to help. His last message said he'd contact us as soon as he finishes the cleanup. There's little point in creating interruptions until then.>

I entered a tight alley between two butcher shops.

Lights hung from coat hangers, electric cords snaking in every direction. Freezers chugged and clanked. I stepped through fluorescent puddles of refrigerant that mingled with ice melt. My nose wrinkled at the reek of blood as butchers cleaved and sawed through bone and sinew. Glass cases showed off the rare and expensive prime cuts while the cheap stuff—the lab-grown meat pastes—sat in iced buckets labeled with hand-written signs advertising two credits per scoop.

The narrow alley opened up into a wide square. Plastic tables and chairs sat under dim lights. The outer perimeter was jammed with grills and griddles, rice makers and woks. Thanks to orbiting agriculture platforms, the food situation had improved a bit in recent years. Perhaps the only bright spot in our blighted existence.

Reaching the *BENTOS* cart, I bought the special of the day, white rice with fried protein paste and a potato slaw. A woman hurried from the back to wipe a table for me. Thanks to the sandstorms whipped up by the terraforming project, it was a constant challenge to keep anything on Mars dust free.

I took a seat and set Nigel on the table. I peeled the bag open enough to give him a view, but decided against pulling him all the way out for fear of attracting stares.

“You okay?” I asked.

“I’m fine. Being carried in a sack is a humiliation I’ll gladly survive. Is it too early to see if anybody contacted that ghost account?”

"Hasn't happened yet, but Smith will let me know when it does." I pulled the lid off my sectioned tray deciding to dig into the dessert first, a sweetened soy curd. After a couple bites, my appetite fully triggered, and I devoured the spicy slaw, realizing I hadn't eaten in more than a day.

<Did you ID the bodies?>

<Yes, facial recognition IDed three people we didn't already know about. I can't help you with the ones who were beheaded.>

<Who are they?>

<The first, Hans Gottberg, was a beggar who worked Red Tunnel. The second, Sheila Bartolo, had several arrests for possession with intent to sell. The third, Thelma Kotto, worked for the Church of Mars.>

<The church? What did she do?>

<She was a priest.>

Strange. Until now, it seemed that Robbins avoided selecting anybody with a high profile, which befitted an operation that sought to avoid attention. After a few more bites of my food, I told Smith to call Hennessey again.

He sighed.

<Did you really just do that?> I clicked my chopsticks. <When I give you an order, you do what I say, got it?>

<If you insist,> he said. After a few seconds, he said, <He's not responding. Would you like me to connect you to his AI, Thomas?>

<No, that's okay,> I said. But it wasn't okay. Something was wrong.

The Peerless Leader wouldn't refuse my call. A bug had built a secret lab. The shapeshifter had kidnapped human subjects and popped their heads like they were cans of tomatoes. A human brain had been transplanted into an alien.

Me ringing Hennessey was not a casual call. The lab cleanup and cover story was a high stakes operation, and I sure as hell wasn't going to talk to some program that liked to be called Thomas. For some reason, Smith still had a soft spot for Hennessey's AI, but I'd been burned by Thomas before. Never trust an AI that isn't your own.

I scarfed down the last of my food and grabbed the bag with Nigel inside. Something was off, and I knew exactly where I needed to go.

CHAPTER NINE

<DENVER? WHERE ARE YOU GOING?>

I ignored the voice rattling in my head. I knew he'd object. As always, he wanted to protect me, but I wasn't going to let him talk me out of it. Hennessey had gone incommunicado, and I was going to find out what the hell was going on.

I turned into the same alley I had when following Lucas Robbins. The metalworks shop stood at the end.

<I really don't think this is a good idea, Denver. You don't know who might be in there.>

Passing the wide-eyed stares of some of the same vendors I'd aggressively questioned not long ago, I marched up to the door and pulled it wide. Stepping inside, I saw it looked the same as it had the last time I was here. Sparks fireworked from welding guns. Robotic lasers moved too fast for my eyes to track. The air was oven hot, my palm starting to sweat where I held the handles of Nigel's bag.

I moved the bag to my left hand and took Smith with my right. The brick wall was still there, and I used a toe to push the same stone I had the last time. The wall swung open and I stepped into the lab, a waft of cold air washing over me.

I was in the same room as before. It had the same dimensions, but everything else was different. Instead of bodies hanging from hooks, I saw shelves packed with bolts of white cloth. In place of lab tables were sewing machines.

I checked the door behind me to verify I hadn't taken a wrong turn. Looking down, I toed a bloodletting floor gutter. This was the same room.

The floor drain was hidden by silky fabrics rippling from spools to be gobbled up by the machines. Robotic arms folded and pinched while sewing needles pistoned up and down at dizzying speed. Fabric spat back out from the far end of the assembly before getting sliced by giant guillotines.

I scanned the room's perimeter to verify no one else was here.

"Can I see?" asked Nigel.

Tucking Smith away, I took Nigel from his bag, gripping his hair gladiator style.

"This the place?" he asked.

"It is."

Wheeled robots cycled around the room, first feeding fabric into the machinery, then retrieving the final product from the other end. By the looks of it, the equipment was programmed to make robes, the same kind of robes worn by the CoMers.

I stepped past some shelves to stand on the exact spot where I left the splattered alien remains. No black goo on the floor. No evidence of the violence that occurred here. "Hennessey did a hell of a job," I said, speaking loud enough to be heard over the machinery.

Stress melted from my shoulders. The Peerless Leader came through after all. I shouldn't have had any doubts. Smith was right, Hennessey was just too busy to keep me in the loop. He'd call as soon as he could to let me know how the cover story would go.

I wandered into different stacks of fabric, likely intended for bedsheets or window coverings. Every color of the rainbow was surely represented, but to my eyes they were all one shade of gray or another. Though the color was lost, I could still appreciate the patterns, so many of them inspired by Earth's almost-dead natural world. Flowers and trees. Birds and butterflies.

I felt a tug near my hip. Before I could react, Smith was yanked from my holster and sent flying into a bin of scrap cloth. Heart kicking into gear, I swung around, whipping Nigel's head like a mace. Failing to make contact, I cocked a fist before freezing at the sight of a pulseripper lined up on my chest.

"Don't move," she said. Her hair was shaved, and rows of tattooed numbers covered most of her face. She held the pulseripper steady, like it wasn't her first time.

Adrenaline surged through my system. I could taste metal in my mouth. Yet, I fought to stay still, breath raking in and out, every ounce of my being urging fight or flight.

<I've patched into your eyes, Denver,> said Smith. <Keep calm. If she wanted to shoot you, she would've done it already.>

<Where did she come from?>

<I assume the door.>

<No shit. You didn't see her?>

<Not until I went flying. I figured it was you pulling me from the holster or I would've zapped her.>

<Any idea what the numbers on her face mean?>

<They look like coordinates.>

<To where?>

<Running a scan now.>

The woman was still measuring me with her eyes, a pair of dark puddles over sunken cheeks.

<I can't find a match for the coordinates anywhere on Mars,> said Smith.

<Check Earth.>

<Negative. If they are coordinates, they're from the other side of the galaxy.>

Her gaze flicked over to Nigel, thin eyebrows puzzling up.

"Who the bloody hell are you?" asked Nigel.

She didn't look amused. "The one with the gun asks the questions," she said before turning her gaze back on me. "What's your name?"

"Denver Moon. Who are you?"

"You're Denver Moon?" Her tone said she was unimpressed. "I guess I should've figured that out when I saw that Earth shooter on your hip."

<Hear that, Denver? I'm more famous than you now.>

Without thinking, I rolled my eyes. The woman noticed. "Got a problem?"

"No, no problem," I said.

"Don't be so nervous," she said. "I hear we're playing for the same team."

"What team is that? You work for the church?"

"The Church of Mars? No, I don't. I heard you were here. . .before. You know what this place was."

I narrowed my eyes. "You heard I was here? You're one of them, aren't you? You ran this lab."

I looked deep into her eyes, searching for a trace of the flicker that only the alien optics possessed—something that only my colorblind eyes could see, but there was nothing there.

"I didn't have anything to do with that madness," she said.

"But you cleaned it up. You put all this equipment in here."

She casually swept the gun in the direction of the machinery. "I did a pretty good job, don't you think?"

I should've been relieved to no longer have a pulseripper trained on my heart, but my nerves were wound so tight, I could barely process what she'd said. After a long pause, I pulled a thread from my foggy thoughts. "You said you don't work for the church. The church was supposed to clean this place up."

"You should go," she said as she trained her weapon back on me.

"Can I get my gun?"

"You can get it slow, and you can keep your hands high after you put it in your holster."

I turned Nigel to face me. "Sorry," I said. "I have to put you away."

"I'd nod if I could," he said.

I put Nigel's head back into his bag and took a step toward the scrap bin to collect Smith. But then I stopped and turned back to her. "No." I said, and I crossed my arms. "I'm not leaving. Not until you tell me who you are, and who you work for. Not until you tell me who was running that freakshow of a lab."

"What makes you think I won't just shoot you? I could incinerate your body just like I did the other corpses."

"You said we're on the same team, and you don't look foolish enough to harm an ally whose only sin is asking a few questions."

Her eyes locked on mine and a small smirk emerged. "Such a stubborn little girl."

At first, I thought I hadn't heard right, but she'd spoken plenty clear. She couldn't have said anything else. My knees wobbled, and I had to lock my legs to keep upright. I stepped toward her, the pulseripper completely forgotten in my mind. "What did you call me?"

"You heard me," she said.

I pointed a finger at her. "That's what my grandfather used to call me. How do you know him?"

"It's time for you to go."

My head was swimming. No, not swimming. It was sinking, plunging to the murky depths. Questions fired fast in my mind. How was my grandfather involved? Who was this woman? Who ordered her to clean this place? Where the hell was Hennessey? He was the one I told Smith to message. He was the one who was supposed to take care of this mess.

Numb, I went to the bin and pulled Smith from the pile of scrap material. Slowly, I tucked him into his holster. As ordered, I raised both hands. Nigel's head hung close to my face, his features partly visible through the thin plastic bag. Feeling completely lost, I found my way to the door.

She stopped me with a shout over the drone of machinery. "I hear you're going after Rafe Ranchard," she said.

I didn't respond. Didn't even turn back to look at her,

but I did freeze right where I was. How did she know so much when I knew so little?

Her voice was calm. Matter-of-fact. "Bishop Ranchard worked for Blevin's Mine before he went back to the church."

I nodded without looking back. It was in Blevin's Mine that he'd tried to kill me.

"That's their ore that they use in the shop up front."

The latest piece of information stuck in my head like a bone in a meat grinder. My mind was so jammed up, I couldn't process all of the implications. But one big revelation struck like a thunderclap.

I wasn't working two cases anymore. Rafe Ranchard and this abomination of a lab were connected. The link might be thin, thin as a thread of spider web, but the connection was there, and I knew deep down in my gut that the link would only get stronger.

No, I wasn't working two cases anymore. I was working one.

CHAPTER TEN

NEEDING A REST FROM CARRYING NIGEL around, I'd left his head in my apartment. I slipped my other partner into his holster and pulled my longcoat over him, keeping him hidden from view.

Stepping around a bend, I tacked onto the lineup outside the Syrtus Major Planum Cathedral, the second largest church in Mars City. Although it was only a coincidence that it had been named for Mars' dark spot, I thought it a fitting name for the black-hearted Rafe Ranchard's parish.

The queue was surprisingly long for a midnight service. I stood behind a group of silk-robed monks, their shaved heads reflecting the light of the torch-lined tunnel. Lanterns hung from the ceiling, their flames close enough to warm my cheeks as the line inched forward.

Behind me was a young couple, each of them wearing miner uniforms. I didn't make eye contact. Nearing the entrance, I put on a hat to keep my face in shadow. I didn't need anybody noticing me as I watched Rafe's sermon. This was a mission to gather information. Nothing more.

<Denver? I just managed to breach the records you wanted. It wasn't an easy hack.>

<Summarize.>

<The tattooed woman in the lab was right. The metal-works shop uses ore mined almost exclusively from Blevin's Mine, a subsidiary of Stanislaw Corp.>

<Whose name is on the shop's lease?>

<Going back two years, the signatures all belong to Rafe Ranchard.>

I had to shake my head, still floored by the idea that Rafe was connected to the lab. Whoever the tattooed woman was, she'd given me the tip of the year.

<Did you make copies of those docs?>

<Indeed, I did,> said Smith.

<Send a message to Hennessey. Tell him we need to talk. Tell him Rafe is a bug lover, and I can prove it.>

<Message sent.>

I could hardly believe my good luck. All I had to do was show that documentation to the Peerless Leader, and it would be more than enough to get Rafe excommunicated. The public may never learn what happened in that lab, but once Hennessey realized Rafe was conspiring with aliens, he'd find any excuse he could to kick Rafe out on his ass.

In fact, I was surprised it hadn't happened already.

Thomas, Hennessey's AI, had a network vaster and better connected than Smith, which meant Hennessey should already know whose name was on the lease.

I stepped over the stone threshold into the cathedral and made for a pew in the back of the cavernous main hall. Taking a seat at the end of the hard-backed bench, I kept my head down to hide my smile. The job Jard hired me for was good as done. Who would've thought it could be so easy? The wheels of Rafe's demise had been set in motion the moment I informed Hennessey about the bodies in that lab. My work was finished before I ever set foot in Jard's office.

But that didn't mean I could relax anytime soon. Rafe's role and motivations were still a mystery, and I couldn't let my guard down until the full plot was exposed and the alien experiments came to a halt.

I looked up at the glass ceiling towering far overhead. The sight was stunning. Bright light filtered through a complex pattern of prisms to illuminate the rotunda with a kaleidoscopic weave of beams. I could only imagine how hypnotic it would be in color.

The cathedral was probably at three-quarters capacity and still filling. I kept to myself, my eyes on the altar, waiting for Rafe's sermon to begin. The altar stood twenty feet off the floor. The spiral staircase that led up to it was made of glass so as to be invisible to all but the first few rows. The illusion of the floating altar was enhanced by burning incense that bathed the staircase in a cloud.

A group of priests appeared on a balcony and the crowd quickly hushed. The priests began to chant, their voices syncing into a deep drone. One of the priests, a woman with long braids, jumped the balcony wall and fell a few feet before unseen cables hoisted her up. The other priests followed, all of them eerily holding prayer poses as their chants continued.

I turned my eyes back to the altar, and Rafe was already there. My heart jumped at the sight of him. His head and face had been shaved since the last time I'd seen him. A thick neck disappeared into the folds of a silk robe that covered every other inch of his body, even his hands. He seemed to glimmer amongst all the beams of light.

The bastard was going down, of that I was sure. But so many questions still remained, and the first one I needed to answer was why. Why did Rafe help the aliens by giving them a space to carry out their experiments? Had he made the same treasonous deal as my grandfather? The thought made me ill. The alien threat was dire enough without us turning against ourselves.

The chants silenced, and the crowd moved to their knees, myself included. Rafe spread his arms wide, the shape of his hands visible through his draping sleeves.

A dozen gargoyle statues appeared around him. Where they'd come from, I could only guess. Upon a closer look, I saw they were human instead of the otherworldly creatures of ancient Earth. But that didn't make them any less sinister. One had clawed out its own heart.

Another was chewing on a dismembered arm. A third had driven a knife into her ear. Horror after horror, I recognized them as the feve-stricken souls the church was originally formed to prevent.

I didn't even hear Rafe's first words. I was too disgusted by his brazen hypocrisy. How dare he use the terrors of red fever to his own benefit when he was allied with the very aliens causing it? Gods, I was going to enjoy watching him fall.

"We are destroyers," he said, a fist showing through his sleeve, his voice tinged with fire. "Everything we touch turns to ash. We murdered one planet, and now we've started to strangle a second. Our minds are weak. Addled. Stricken with fever. Rotten like dropped fruit infested by worms. This is who we are."

All around me, people nodded in agreement. <A little dramatic, don't you think, Smith? How do people buy this crap?>

<What can I say? They've become cynical. Their lives are bleak and filled with fear. In times like these, the message doesn't matter as much as the messenger. They'll believe anything that comes off the tongue of somebody who promises to deliver them from their pain.>

I wanted to argue, but I had no words. Every once in a while, Smith proved wiser than anybody else in my life, and that included the grandfather whose memories formed most of his personality. Though I wasn't sure he'd appreciate it, I patted his handle through my coat. His testiness toward me bringing Nigel on board was off target. He should know he could never be replaced.

Rafe held his followers with a stare. "We, us, our very selves, are sin incarnate. But that doesn't mean we aren't capable of beauty and grace. It was a divine moment when we created them. Our children. Our better selves. The botsies.

"Don't you see what an amazing accident they were? The inventors wanted to create robots. Tools. Slaves. But in the process, they programmed the botsies to be pure. To be without sin. Without even realizing it, they created a race unburdened by our frailties."

<Denver?>

<Yes?>

<The anonymous account we set up and gave to the monk outside Jard's received a message.>

<Read it to me.>

<Meet at the Earth Park. Tomorrow. Sunset.>

The Earth Park. The message didn't have to say more. Mars only had one park.

<Think it's from Rafe himself?> I asked.

<It came in shortly before he started talking, so it could be. Should I confirm the meeting?> asked Smith.

I thought for a minute before saying no. <I've already got Rafe dead to rights. It's not worth the risk to send Nigel in undercover.>

Rafe was talking about the evils of botsie parlors now. He used words like loathsome and monstrous to describe botstringers like Jard. His radical remedies included words like blood and burn and raze. As far as I knew, the plight of the botsies was the only thing he really cared about, the only common thread between his last stint in the church and this one. I'd moved a lot closer to his position on that issue over the last year, but his righteous tone had crossed the line into a militancy that filled me with dread. It was only a matter of time before he or one of his followers lit a match that couldn't be put out.

I didn't need to hear any more. I stood and headed for the exit, but the going was slow as the back of the church was jammed with people who had arrived too late to get a seat.

<Where are you going?> asked Smith.

<It's time to talk to Hennessey,> I said as I picked my way into the crowd. <Time to put an end to Rafe's bullshit.>

<But—?>

<No buts,> I interrupted. <I'm going to walk right into his church and insist I get to see him. I'll wait all night if I have to.>

I made it to the door, eager to get out of this place, but then I heard something that made me stop. I turned around to face Rafe. Leaning to my right, I could just see the bishop through a sliver in the crowd.

Even though he couldn't see me, couldn't possibly be able to pick me out of this tight mass of his true believers, I still felt like he was looking right at me. Both of his robe-covered hands were on his heart, his head tilted just enough to make him look troubled. Yet, his voice lacked even the slightest hint of concern.

"The Peerless Leader is deathly ill," he said to a chorus of gasps. "I fear he might not have much time left on this world."

CHAPTER ELEVEN

"ARE YOU SURE YOU WANT TO DO THIS?"

"It's my job now. A big improvement over my last one if you ask me," said Nigel, his head lying on its side atop my kitchen counter.

"It will be a big risk."

"I know, but if Bishop Ranchard is as dangerous a bloke as you say, he has to be stopped."

I smiled. "I knew you would be a good hire."

An undercover job wasn't exactly the patty-cake assignment I wanted to give to a rookie, but Nigel and I had already been through some firefights together. If anybody could handle it, he could. I picked him up and put him into a backpack.

The infiltration of Ranchard's inner circle was back on. I had plenty of evidence that Rafe was conspiring with the aliens who ran that atrocity of a lab, but who was I going to bring it to? Hennessey, the one person I could trust to do something about it was sick. Deathly ill, according to Rafe, which finally explained why the Peerless Leader wasn't responding to my requests.

Deep down, I knew Hennessey's illness was somehow Rafe's doing. The timing of it stank worse than a sulfur bath. Gods, what if Rafe had intercepted my message to Hennessey? Rafe is a bug lover, and I can prove it. It couldn't have been more than fifteen minutes later that Rafe publicly announced Hennessey's illness.

I went out the door. The tulou was quiet this time of the AM. Too late for rush hour. But still too early for the overnight shifters to come home. Thirty levs deep, the complex was shaped like a giant missile silo, homes dug all around its rock walls. Stepping along the ring-shaped walkway, I passed open windows, the sound of clacking dishes or holo-vid systems or, in one case, a crying baby.

<How exactly do you think you're going to hand off Nigel to Rafe's people tonight? What if it's Rafe himself who does the pickup in the Earth Park? He can't know it's you planting Nigel into his cadre of botsie asylum seekers or whatever they are.>

I started up a set of stairs. <Agreed. I need somebody to make the drop, somebody Rafe doesn't know. I also need a way for Nigel and I to communicate once he's inside.>

<He has a comm system built-in.>

<I know, but we know damn well how prone to paranoia Rafe is. There's no way he's going to bring Nigel into

his fold without monitoring or disabling his communications. We need a stealth transmission system he won't find.>

<I bet I can guess where you're heading.>

<I bet you can too.> I turned for the tram system.

The tunnel was dark, hardly a third of the lights were actually working, and those that were barely oozed enough light to keep me from hitting the walls. <Are you sure this is the right way? I can't see shit.>

<I'm sure. I know the lighting is weak, but it's more than sufficient for an able-eyed person.>

I refrained from a terse *what's that supposed to mean*? I knew what he meant. My vision was degenerating. Mars' atmosphere was bad enough for human eyes, but my particular flavor of monochromism often resulted in blindness by middle age. My grandfather was still beating the odds, but Smith kept insisting I wasn't going to be so lucky. He was wrong. <I can see fine. It's just dark down here.>

<I looked up an appointment with a good doctor,> said Smith. <Can I book it?>

<No, dammit. I just said I can see well enough.>

<The doctor won't even need to touch you. All she'll do is go over some options. Synth eyes and augments aren't that expensive anymore.>

<No appointments. I like my vision the way it is.>

<Your eyes are not magical, you know. I've never been able to confirm you can really spot aliens.>

<No appointment, and that's final.> I didn't care if he didn't believe me. I knew what I saw.

The first time was when I first met Doctor Werner. I saw a flash in his eyes, and I saw the same thing days later in Bow, the alien spying on the church. I couldn't see the flash all the time, only when the lighting was blinking or shifting. But when I did, it was unmistakable. Their eyes glowed like those of an animal caught in a beam of light. As far as I knew, it was the only way to tell the shapeshifters apart from us humans. Maybe a doctor or a scientist could do it with something as simple as an X-ray or blood sample, but that would require capture and experimentation. To this point, very few people knew about the aliens. And those who did wouldn't dare try anything for fear the aliens might just decide extermination was a better path for humans than enslavement.

<Take the corridor on the right.>

I did, but I mistook the corner for a shadow and bumped my shoulder on the wall as I entered. Hoping he didn't notice, I kept walking like nothing happened.

<My vibration sensors detected that.>

<Shut up.>

I stopped at a door, looked left and right to confirm we were alone. We were deep under the surface, about as deep as you could go. These levs were built for a great influx of immigrants who never came. Earth was a dying hell but getting to Mars wasn't cheap, and the horrors of red fever didn't do much for tourism. Now these levs were mostly empty except for squatters and criminals.

We were alone. I pulled Smith from his holster, and just like he did a year ago, he zapped the lock and I heard a click. I pushed the door open and stepped inside. The battery-driven lights flicked on automatically.

The room was just as I remembered it except the two tangled bodies on the floor had been removed. Stieg and Ana.

The easel and chair were still there, and I walked up to look at the painting Stieg had been crafting on the last day of his life. A heavy blanket of sadness settled over me as I studied his work. My arms and legs felt heavy as my weighing heart. The painting wasn't complete, but Stieg had a talent for capturing people. That was what I thought of her now. Ana. A person.

But she wasn't human. She was a botsie, her naked body a quilt of mismatched parts that somehow combined to make her look beautiful. It was tragic what happened here. Topping a list of my regrets—and I've gathered quite a few—this was it. I'd replayed the events a million times over, and it always ended the same way, with Ana and Stieg dead on the floor.

I set my backpack down and reached inside to pull Nigel out, but when his skin felt slick, I jerked my hand away. "What the hell?"

A muffled voice came from inside the bag. "It's bloody hot in here."

I grabbed him by the hair and pulled him free. "You can sweat? Why?"

"Many of my former customers liked it," he said. "It's scented like a fine English cologne."

"That it is," I said upon catching a noseful of musky odors. "Can you turn it on and off?"

"Of course. Except when I'm severely overheated, it kicks in automatically to see if it can bring my temperature to an acceptable level, assuming I have enough coolant in my skull reserves. If not, my emergency systems will trigger a complete shutdown. Thankfully, since the backup batteries in my head don't have much to power, I should be good for a while. At least until you can give me a proper charge."

"So, you're saying you liked the shopping bag better than the backpack?"

"Quite right." Nigel's eyes wandered the room. "What is this place?"

"This is where the last case I worked for Jard ended. We need to get you installed with a secondary transmission system."

I carried him past a workbench to a set of shelves stocked with spare parts. A box was filled with robotic fingers, another with toes. Partial arms and legs sat on the floor, wires sprouting like weeds from the ends.

"Bollocks," said Nigel.

"What?"

"I was hoping to spot a spare torso. If we could find one in this mess, there might be enough to cobble me a new body."

<Testing, one, two, three.>

"I hear you," said Nigel.

"How's the feed, Smith?" I said aloud.

<I see everything Nigel sees.>

"Good," I stood and stretched my back after hours hunched over the workbench. "Now send the feed to me."

Smith tapped me into Nigel's new microcam, and I had to blink as vision blossomed with color. My normally snowy world of slate and granite dripped with honey hues as I studied a close-up of myself from Nigel's perspective. The shadowy bags under my eyes were a faint shade of purple. Not too bad considering the mess I'd become over the last six months, but all-in-all, I thought I looked better in black-and-white. Stepping back, the overhead lights had chilled from a hot white to an icy blue fluorescence that made my bleached hair glow. I saw the streaks of rusty dirt on the walls now.

As was common with the instances Smith would tap into my optics feed and stream color right into my retinas, I was hit with a dizzying sense of motion sickness. I tried to blink it away and prepared myself for the inevitable headache.

"What time is it?"

<It's almost an hour to sundown.>

"I hear when Smith talks too," said Nigel. "Smith, we've never been able to talk directly before. It's good to meet you, mate."

<Yes,> said Smith, his voice cold as a dead fish.

Nigel didn't seem to notice. "I really think this is going to work, Smith. You made the right choice installing the transmitter the way you did."

<Yes,> said Smith.

Through Nigel's eyes, I saw myself frowning at Smith's cold shoulder act, which meant he could see it too. "That's enough," I said. "You can disconnect the stream."

On cue, my brain flipped channels, and I was back to seeing through my own eyes. The rich world of color and spice was gone, my spectrum replaced by that of an old-Earth newspaper.

<Back to normal?>

<Confirmed.> Though he'd complained the whole time, Smith did a nice job of talking me through a series of procedures. To provide two-way communication, we salvaged a transmitter from a spare botsie head and embedded it inside Nigel's nose. Reclaiming a digicam from an eyeball, I installed it behind his left retina so we could see and hear anything in his immediate vicinity. The only thing that had me worried was the wireless connection between the new microgear and Nigel's chip. We'd hidden the connection as deep as we could inside

Nigel's software stack, but the connection was there and a deep diagnostic would pick it up if anybody thought to run one. Staying connected to Nigel this way was risky, but there was no way to avoid it if I wanted to maintain the ability to communicate.

A knock sounded on the door. Knowing she wouldn't hear me through the heavy steel, I went to the door and pulled it open. "Navya," I said.

"How are you, Denver?"

"Come." I pulled her into an embrace. "Thanks for coming. We need your help."

"You know you can call me anytime, right?" She pulled back from my arms. "We've been friends since we were kids. You don't have to wait until you need something."

"I know. You're right. I've been struggling of late. I'm still...still..."

"Struggling with the loss of Ojiisan? You know he's not dead, right? It's not too late to reconcile."

I escorted her into the room. The first thing she noticed was the painting, and she went to the easel. "Wow," she said, "was this done with real paint? Who's the botsie?"

"She's from a case I worked last year."

Navya looked at me like she was waiting for me to elaborate.

"It went bad," I said. I didn't know what else to offer.

She studied the painting a while longer before

lightening the mood with a shy smile. "Speaking of botsies," she leaned close. "Where's Nigel?"

"Are you blushing?"

"Well, you said he'd be here, and we've had some, some..."

"Some what?" I played dumb.

"You know...We've had some... fun. So, I thought maybe..."

"I'm pretty sure you're turning red as a Martian sunset," I said with a grin.

"Well," she tugged at the zipper of her flight suit to reveal some lacey black lingerie. "I brought something special, and I thought that maybe after I help you out, he and I—"

I put up a hand to stop her there, but before I could speak, Nigel's voice came from the table against the wall. "Sounds like a jolly good time, love, but as you can see, I seem to have lost the good stuff."

Navya spun around, her eyes landing on his smiling head.

"What?" She sucked in a breath and a hand snapped to cover her mouth. "What happened?" Her voice jumped more than an octave.

"I never got fixed after getting shot."

"How could you?" said Navya with maximum indignance.

It took me a moment to realize she was looking at me when she said that. "Don't blame me," I said with a little indignation of my own. "Jard's the one who never repaired him."

"He got shot saving you, Denver. Not Jard."

Nigel laughed. "She's got you there, boss."

CHAPTER TWELVE

STIEG'S PAINTING OF ANA WAS NESTLED UNDER my arm as I walked a stone path that weaved through thick grass swaying in a light breeze. It was too beautiful to leave behind. Countless leaves rustled overhead, permitting speckles of light to peek through the canopy and momentarily catch a fern here or a flower there. In the distance, I noticed a thicket of Yoshino trees, their cherry blossoms in full bloom. The air smelled of a fresh green my eyes couldn't begin to perceive. I stepped off the trail, my boots crunching over a patch of dirt to release the scent of rich loam.

Was this really what it was once like on Earth? Was Japan like this, where the samurai of old could climb a forested mountain or ride a horse through thickets of bamboo? Where a young girl could climb a hill and see domeless landscapes for kilometers? Where there were no sandstorms cutting visibility or peppering your faceplate? Where air and water and life itself were abundant?

I passed a flowerbed, my nostrils filling with such sweet botanical fragrance, I wanted to stop and never take another step. Mars' one and only park—tucked high in the upper domes where the elite live—was so beautiful it hurt. So beautiful it should be packed with people all hours of the day. But it wasn't, and I knew why. It was the same reason I tried to stay away. The aftereffect.

The wondrousness of living scenery was a blessing, but limited resources meant this park was the only one like it on all of Mars. There were few things as emotionally satisfying as walking the scenic pathways, but at some point, I'd have to leave and go back to our world of stone and steel filled to the brim with artificial tastes, sights and smells. And when I did, the tunnels I called home would never appear hollower. Come this time tomorrow, I'd be experiencing a deep longing, so deep I'd feel it in my marrow. It was always the same. Every time I came here, I was damning myself to a bleak, dark emptiness that would last for days or weeks. It was the curse of all Martians to wear a heavy cloak of crushing sadness for the world we'd lost.

I pinned the painting under my arm and hopped across a small brook. To catch my balance, I grabbed a tree trunk with my free hand. I held on longer than I needed and embraced the rough bark under my fingers. It felt so right, so elemental, that it threatened to bring tears to my eyes. Same for the butterfly kiss of leaves on my cheek as I ducked through a thicket. With every step, I reveled in the soft cushion of turf under my heels. This was what Mars could be one day. We weren't meant to live like rats. This was why we needed the aliens' help no matter the risks. We didn't have the technology to transform this world from red to green on our own.

I scrambled up a grassy hill and made my way toward the observation tower. Up its steps was the best view in Mars City. From there, I'd be able to see Navya and Nigel, whom I'd left waiting on a bench near the central fountain. I started up the stairs, climbing until I reached the top, my head standing just a few feet under the domed ceiling.

I propped the painting against a rail and took a deep breath. My eyes wandered the narrow vista. To the left was the stand of trees I'd passed through, oaks and maples and elms. To the right was a small orchard of pear and apple. Straight ahead, a shimmering pond invited me to splash in its waters.

Though I'd stood here many times before, the view was so stunning, I just about asked Smith to colorize it for me. But seeing it in full color was too painful to think about. Better to dull the impact by enjoying it in black and white. Better still to enjoy it in a picture like the habit of most Martians.

The fountain was close enough that I could see the shapes of koi moving under the water's surface. Navya sat right where I'd left her, a bag on her lap with Nigel's head inside. <This better work,> I said.

<I don't see why it won't,> said Smith. <As long as Navya sticks to the plan, there's no reason why Rafe, or whoever he sends in his place, won't believe it. The security camera I tapped is showing three people who just entered.>

<Where?>

<You should be able to see them in three, two, one…>

Two men and a woman came into view. The woman walked slowly in a tight-fitting white gown. One of the men, dressed in a tuxedo, carried the tail of her dress to keep it off the ground. The other man carried a tripod. <Wedding photos.>

<So it appears.>

I looked up at the glass ceiling, at a sky that should be brilliant blue but wasn't, and not because I was color-blind. Dirtied by the solar system's largest dust devil, the sky was a dark and angry mass of swirling sand and grit.

Still, the fact that the stormy view was starting to blacken told me the sun was going down. Nearly sunset.

I scanned the area, looking for anybody in a church robe, spotting one near the English garden. <See him?>

<I do,> said Smith. <He must've been here before we arrived.>

<Identify.>

A moment of lag went by before Smith beamed a zoomed image of the monk's face into my mind. It was him. The botsie I'd talked to outside Jard's place. A surge of confidence welled inside. Navya would turn Nigel over to him. The monk would bring him into Rafe's church. And finally, I'd learn everything I needed to know about Rafe and whatever schemes he was running.

Navya spotted the monk and pulled the bag open so Nigel would be visible to her arrived visitor.

<Patch me in,> I said before grabbing the railing against the wave of dizziness that was sure to strike.

Smith did as ordered, and a disorienting flash preceded my new upside-down view from Nigel's eyes. I wobbled a bit but held on as I watched the monk peer into the bag.

"Cheers," said Nigel.

The monk turned to Navya. "You're not her. You're not the one who stole him from the botstringer."

"She couldn't make it," said Navya. "She asked me to come in her place."

As we'd agreed, Navya set the bag containing Nigel on the bench and abruptly stood up. Without saying another word, she walked away. Smith flipped me back to my own eyes so I could see her go for the closest exit. The monk would take Nigel or he wouldn't, but we weren't going to let him ask any more questions.

The monk watched her for a bit. Then he took the bag and strode in the opposite direction.

I smiled. Mission accomplished.

I grabbed the painting and was about to go back down the stairs when a voice made me freeze.

"Denver," was the only word he said.

CHAPTER THIRTEEN

<THIS IS BAD,> SAID SMITH. HE RECOGNIZED THE voice too. <Real bad.>

I stayed where I was, my fingers gripping the canvas frame so tight it hurt. Without turning around, I worked to calm my racing heart. "What are you doing here, Rafe?"

"Same as you," he said. "Perching on the high ground to watch the transaction. You never know when somebody might be setting a trap. A detective should've predicted you might have company on this tower. Now turn around slow, and don't you dare reach for that damn gun on your hip."

Slowly, I released the painting and turned with my hands out front. Ranchard was in his robes, baggy silks covering every inch of him except for a shadowed face peeking out from under his hood. My eyes trailed downward to a small barrel protruding from behind the silk near his right hand. No doubt a pulseripper.

<I don't have a shot,> said Smith. <Not while I'm in your holster. The best I can do is an EM blast, which might be enough to scramble the electronics on his gun. At best, it would buy you a couple seconds.>

My finger was already twitching. I could end this right now. Let them lock me up for murder if that was what it came to. I couldn't let Rafe take over the church. He leased that lab to those alien bastards. Innocent-until-proven-guilty was a luxury for a bygone age. He was a bug sympathizer, and I couldn't let him become the most powerful man on Mars. A hatred I'd never known was surging through my nervous system. <Do it. Let's waste this asshole.>

<No, Denver, you don't understand. The EM blast will scramble my signals too. I won't be able to target or fire. The pulse is intended to buy you time to run for it.>

<Screw that. I can take him. Right here. Right now.> I changed the angle of my hand. Moved my fingers into position for a quick snatch.

Rafe's eyes caught the movement and zeroed in on my right hand, waiting for me to make my move. The smug bastard was grinning. He wanted to kill me as bad as I wanted to kill him.

It was time to end this, old-west style. Him or me. All of Mars—all of humanity—came down to this one moment. I'd draw and dive at the same time. Smith's targeting system would have no problem adjusting to the movement. We'd blow a hole the size of Jard's fat fists right through his chest.

<Don't do this, Denver. You're not fast enough. You'll be dead before you catch hold of my grip.>

I couldn't wait to see the expression on Rafe's face when the giant gaping hole finally made him realize he wasn't the gods' chosen one. When he realized he was nothing but another delusional asshole.

Rafe's grin had morphed into a sneer. If I didn't draw soon, he might just take the initiative.

I could do this. Quick grab. Dive left. Fire.

<He's not me,> said Smith.

The words froze in my mind. I couldn't begin to process what Smith meant, but there was something in his tone, something in the way he mimicked my grandfather's voice right then that gave me pause.

<I know you don't like it when I call myself Ojiisan, but I carry the person you planted inside me. He's the one who betrayed you. Rafe Ranchard isn't him. Rafe isn't me. He isn't the one who betrayed the human race.>

<He's working with the aliens. I know he is.>

<He signed that lease, but we don't know how deep his involvement really is. In the meantime, don't think punishing him will satisfy your desire to punish Ojiisan.>

Rafe's pose held perfectly still, like a cat the instant before it pounces. He didn't blink. Didn't even seem to be breathing. A shiver rippled up my spine. Smith was right.

I had no chance of dropping him before he fired. A deep sigh emerged from tight lungs, and I raised my hands.

Rafe lifted an eyebrow, like he was surprised to see me back down. Breath raked in and out from my chest, adrenaline still coursing through my veins. "No wonder you wear your robes so loose," I said to him. "How would it look for a man who loves the gods as much as you to be carrying a weapon?"

"The gods love those who are smart," he said. "I didn't come here expecting to find you, but I can't say I'm surprised. Best to carry protection, just in case. Don't you think? Never know when I might come face-to-face with a murderer such as you."

"Murderer?"

"I seem to remember you killing some of my miners a year ago."

"Miners? Those were thugs, and that was self-defense."

"Same old Denver. Nothing's ever her fault. I bet you've been that way since the day you were born. Your traitor of a grandfather must've spoiled you rotten."

A reflex buried deep inside wanted to defend the man who raised me. But the truth was the truth. All I could do was keep my hands high and swallow it.

"You should hear how the Peerless Leader talks about him," said Rafe. "He practically froths at the mouth every time the great Tatsuo Moon shows up playing the long-lost hero. If only the people knew what you and I know, that under the surface, he's just a sniveling coward. An alien lover."

"You should talk. I know you're helping them. You leased them the space they used to turn people into lab rats."

"Rats. Isn't that what we all are? Isn't that exactly what the human race is? What else do you call beasts completely consumed with carnal desire and self-interest? Rats or humans, I fail to see the difference."

"But you see the difference between rats and bugs? That's what they are. Bugs who will turn us into mindless drones. They'll make us their slaves."

"Red fever and all that. Yes, the Peerless Leader talks about it all the time. You sound so much more like him than Tatsuo. Are you sure your grandmother didn't start a little something on the side?"

If he was hoping for a reaction, he didn't get one. I glanced over my shoulder to see if the monk was still below, but I saw no sign of him. No sign of Nigel. "Call that botsie monk of yours. Tell him to give me my botsie back."

"Ha! Who else but you would be delusional enough to make demands when staring down a 'ripper. Who are you working for?"

"What makes you think I'm working for anybody? Can't a woman settle her own grudges?"

"I'm told that robot you baited me with is seventeenth

generation. I doubt very much you have the money to own such perfection."

"I've been saving."

"More likely you're working for your old pal Jard Calder. My little protests must really be stinging him in the wallet, eh?" A broad smile stretched across his face. "The botsie trade is going to end, Denver. Wait and see."

"You love botsies so much, give Nigel back. He's a free botsie. He doesn't belong to you."

"Exactly right. They belong to no one but themselves."

"So, you'll let him go?"

"I didn't say that," he said with a self-satisfied wink. "I'm going to talk to him. Whatever his loyalties to you and Jard are, they won't compare to what I can offer."

"And what's that?"

"The future."

"What the hell does that mean?"

"He has a bigger role to play. All botsies who value life and freedom have a destiny to fulfill. Like all the other frees who have come for asylum, he won't be a thing anymore. He won't be a tool. He won't be your tool. He won't be used."

I shook my head. "I'm not using him. He wanted to help me."

Rafe laughed. "You put his head in a bag and handed him off to a stranger so he could be your spy, and you think you're not using him? Come to think of it, you must really think I'm stupid to think a ploy like that would really work."

"You were lucky you came up here later than I did. If you'd gotten here a few minutes earlier, I'd be the one who snuck up behind you."

"Luck? You really believe such things are left to random chance? Yes, the tables would be turned if the timing had been different. But did it ever occur to you that it was the hands of the gods who held me back a minute?"

He stared at me for a long time. Like I was one of his flock. Like his little speech would help me see the light.

"My arms are getting tired," I said. "Are you going to shoot me or what?"

He blinked slowly, like a teacher disappointed by his pupil. "I'm keeping...what did you say his name was? Nigel? He'll stay with the other frees until he's ready to decide his own future."

"And me?"

"It's been fun, our little rivalry," he said, before his voice took on a threatening edge. "But like they say, all good things must come to an end."

<Smith? I think it's time.>

<Get ready to run for the stairs. EM blast in three, two...>

I bent my knees, ready to run barrel straight into him. I'd hit him with everything I had. Hit him with enough force to knock him out of my way before sprinting down the stairs to his rear.

I sucked in a deep breath, ready to rock, but before Smith's countdown made it to one, the gun barrel under Rafe's robe disappeared, and he took a step back toward the stairs.

Smith's countdown stopped. <I don't think he's going to shoot you,> he said. <He must be afraid of witnesses in the park below.>

<That never stopped him before.>

Rafe found the stairs and grabbed the railing with his free hand, which was still under the cover of silk. Wordlessly, he started down, his gaze locked on mine as he took one backwards stair at a time.

"What did you do to Hennessey?" I asked.

Rafe stopped at the first landing. The gun barrel was back, and all it would take was quick twitch of the finger to blow me apart.

<What are you doing?> Smith hissed. <Let him go before he changes his mind!>

I took a step in Rafe's direction, my eyes boring in on his. "What did you do to him?"

"Nothing," he said with a shrug. "Hennessey has gotten old, and so has his rhetoric. Did you know there hasn't been a case of red fever in months? It's time for the church to take a new direction, and that means new leadership."

"I won't let you take over the church. Hennessey is the only one standing between us and the bugs."

"Too late for that, child." He disappeared around the corner.

CHAPTER FOURTEEN

I STOOD UNDER A TREE, A VICIOUS HEADACHE bearing down. I needed a zone in the worst way, but I didn't deserve any form of relief from the mess I'd just created.

I'd lost Nigel. I'd actually lost him.

The communication channel Smith and I worked so hard to install was discovered and disabled before I stepped off of the tower. All Nigel managed to say before the link went dead was, <I'll be okay, Denver. As long as I'm me, I'll learn everything I can.>

<As long as you're you?> I'd said. <What does that mean?>

A response never came. He was gone. He didn't even have a body. No means to defend himself. Jesus, what had I done?

I looked up at the tower. I should've realized Rafe would send somebody up there. I was out of my league. I was a detective. Not an experienced spy who knew how to run a proper operation.

I headed for the exit, my boot heels clopping hollowly against the paved path. The park had closed about five minutes ago. I'd heard the warnings over the loudspeaker, but just couldn't motivate myself to move until now.

Stieg's painting was still in my hand. I'd planned to hang it over the bed. A tribute, I thought. A way to keep his and Ana's memory alive. But the gesture felt empty now that I'd lost Nigel. What was I going to do? Get a picture of Nigel to put on the wall, too? Was that going to be my thing? Keeping mementos of all the lives I'd ruined?

Disgusted, I tossed the art into a flowerbed and kept walking. The dome overhead was now totally dark with night, but the footpath was well lit by ground-level halogens. I passed the koi pond, where Navya had given away Nigel's head. The exit wasn't much farther. She'd be waiting for me there.

But facing her was the last thing I wanted to do. I'd go out that door and have to tell her how badly I'd screwed up.

Instead, I turned around to go through the orchards and out the western exit. Did that make me a bad friend? Guilty as charged.

Nigel's last comments ran through my head over and over as I veered off the path toward the orchards.

As long as I'm me.

Nigel was in Rafe's hands now, and I knew better than to fall for all that freewill bullshit he tried to sell me. He might fancy himself a savior, but a man as controlling and cruel as him was no liberator. Nigel said all he'd needed to let me know Rafe was going to reprogram him, maybe even swap out his chip.

The full weight of Rafe's power grab was finally upon me. He was building an army of botsie drones. Plus, he was well on his way to stealing the church, and with it he'd gain a second army of cultist parasites that he could manipulate and control.

He might be human, but he was just as bad as the alien leader, Doctor Werner.

I entered the shadowy cover of the orchards, my eyes taking a moment to adjust to the darkness. Flowering trees surrounded me. I couldn't tell which were real or synthetic. My nose couldn't determine if they were apple or pear or peach or apricot, but they all smelled of intoxicatingly sweet perfume. The grass was thick underfoot. I wanted to lie down, right here, right now. Wanted to fall asleep and never wake up. If I could, I'd melt into the turf and forget everything that happened and all the ugly things that were still to come.

But I kept walking. I had to get Nigel back. Dammit, I didn't know how, but I had to find a way. The fact that I was working for Jard didn't matter anymore. Rafe Ranchard had to be stopped or he'd soon become the most powerful man on Mars. I still didn't know what kind of deal he'd made with Werner and the other aliens, but anybody who wasn't willing to fight them couldn't be trusted.

This wasn't a case anymore. This was a mission. My mission.

Hennessey might be incapacitated, but as long as he was drawing breath there was a chance that I could restore him to power, and he could set things right.

The sound of a snapping branch came from somewhere behind me. Probably a quick-jabber looking for a discreet place to get high. The park might be closed for the night, but these orchards were a favorite place for addicts, who always managed to find a way to sneak inside. Considering we were in the domes, you'd think their security would be tighter, but the park's founders wanted it to be a place for all. Even what many up here would consider the dregs of society were welcome. Nothing I wasn't used to. I saw more than my fair share of jabbers in the tunnel every day.

I kept moving, my legs gaining purpose the more I thought about taking Rafe down. He'd made a grave mistake letting me live. And I'd do my damnedest to make him realize it.

To my right, from the corner of my eye, I saw something move. Probably just a trick of the light, but that didn't stop my heart from jamming into overdrive. Suddenly, I wanted out of the orchards, wanted out of this place where the darkest shadows hid behind every tree trunk.

I started into a trot and cut to the right, branches slapping at my face.

Footsteps sounded from behind. Lots of them.

<You hear that?> asked Smith.

<I do.>

<Enhanced audio reports at least nine figures matching your pace to the rear.>

And I'd thought Rafe made a mistake letting me live? He'd done nothing of the sort. He just wasn't going to do it himself. Not when we were standing out in the open atop that tower.

<I hear four more,> said Smith. <Thirteen total. The other four are sprinting ahead to flank you from the right.>

I ducked behind a tree and pulled Smith from his holster. <Cannon mode.>

The gun vibrated in my hand, and I heard the low hum as he powered to full. I kept my eyes outward as Smith transformed—through a series of slides, turns, and clicks—from pistol to pulse cannon.

I didn't wait for them to get any closer. I took aim in the general direction of the group of four. If I could make them take cover it might give me time to get out of the orchards and a lot closer to the exit. Get out that exit, and I could escape into any of a dozen tunnels, every one of them packed with people.

Smith bucked in my hands as the pulse fired a warning shot into the trees. Though it was too dark to see, I heard the shattering of timber as the pulse rippled outward. I closed my eyes against a blowback of detritus and sprinted as fast as I dared in the dark, a confetto made of charred leaves peppering my face and arms.

<Trying to make a break for the exit?> asked Smith. <What if they have it covered?>

<Then we're screwed.>

I burst out of the trees and dashed for a dimly-lit bridge. If I could get across it without getting gunned down, I knew there was a gully on the far side where I could hunker long enough to get a few shots off. If I could hold them back, even for a few seconds, it might be enough to make a final sprint out of here.

I could see a little better now that I was out of the woods. I didn't dare tell Smith to turn on a light for fear of broadcasting my position. The bridge was maybe three hundred yards away. I felt a prick in the palm of my hand as Smith injected me with a hefty dose of stims. My vision brightened so much it hurt my eyes, and the entire landscape before me sharpened into supersensitive detail. I could hear everything. The trickle of water from the fountains on the far side of the park. The buzz of insect drones from the orchard I'd abandoned. My skin tingled as if it was charged like an electric fence.

I easily doubled my pace, muscles pumping like an unstoppable locomotive. I was practically flying now, running faster than I'd ever run in my life. Yet, amazingly, my thinking seemed to slow, like I had twice as long for every thought and decision.

Behind me, I heard the stampede of footfalls that had already emerged from the trees. I half-expected to be shot in the back, but considering I hadn't yet, I had to assume they didn't want to attract any attention. The Earth Park might be closed but that didn't guarantee it was empty.

<They're gaining,> said Smith. <Fast.>

Impossible, I thought. Still, I found another gear, my toes barely kissing the ground as I accelerated.

<You won't make it,> said Smith.

I didn't believe him. I was already halfway to the bridge. Nobody could possibly match my speed.

Unless Rafe sent his botsies. <Oh shit, they're botsies.>

<Of course, they are,> said Smith. <What did you expect?>

<You should've told me making a run for it was a dumb plan.>

<If I'd had any better ideas I would have.>

I should've thought it through, but the flight instinct had been too strong. My legs kept pumping. I wanted to stop, turn, and fire, but my amplified hearing told me they were fanned out behind me, all closing in from different angles. There were thirteen of them, and unless they were clustered together, it would take thirteen shots to take them all out. They were so close I doubted

I could get any of them in my sights before they were on top of me.

Something—maybe a fist—slammed my shoulder blade from behind. I began to wobble, but I kept my balance for one stride. Then two. Then I went down, fast and hard.

I bounced off the grass, and pain screamed from every nerve. The stims coursing through my bloodstream couldn't begin to dull the pain as my momentum launched me into a bone-breaking tumble. I felt my wrist give, then an ankle, each snap ringing loud in my hyper-sensitive ears. My left kneecap struck a stone and shattered upon impact.

I hit the ground again, my shoulder taking the brunt and instantly dislocating. The blow forced my chest to compress and snapped three ribs before I ragdolled into another flip. Striking the turf one last time, I skidded to a halt a few feet before the bridge.

Somehow, Smith was still attached to one hand, a broken finger awkwardly poking through the finger guard. One of the botsies was on top of it in an instant, a brutal kick crushing several bones in my hand. Smith flew far out of sight.

I lay on the ground, waves of pain making it impossible to breathe. I should've passed out but the stims wouldn't let me lose consciousness.

Instead, I was trapped in tortuous agony, every one of my senses in complete hyperactive overload. The stims kept me on high alert as my body began to twitch, each tic of a misfiring muscle sending shock waves up and down my spine.

The botsies were all around me, all of them wearing their church silks. I rolled my eyes in every direction, peering through the gaps between them to see if there was any sort of rescue on the way. Maybe I got lucky, and somebody heard the ruckus and called for help. Maybe Navya got concerned and came looking for me.

But I saw nobody. Just a few benches and potted shrubs.

Smith's voice came to me, but it was garbled beyond recognition. Whether it was his circuits or mine that had gotten scrambled I couldn't say. One of the botsies came close, a sinister grin on her face.

I tried to speak but barely managed to move my lips. I tried to sit up but couldn't even lift my shoulders off the ground.

The botsie lifted her robe high enough to expose her feet and sandals. Despite the dim-light, the synth-skin joints of her ankles and toes were visible to my enhanced vision.

She pulled her foot back in preparation for a kick that would take my head off. I didn't flinch or close my eyes. Instead, I wondered why I'd bothered to fight so hard to survive in the first place. Now that the end was here, it didn't seem so bad. Rafe, and the church, and the aliens were somebody else's problem now.

So was Mars.

CHAPTER FIFTEEN

I WAITED FOR THE KICK TO LAND. TO CRUSH MY skull. To rip it free from my spine and send it flying. At least I'd die to the smell of grass and trees instead of dust and sulfur.

A screeching sound clawed at my ears, and a whirl of blinding light whipped across my vision. Reflexively, my hands went to cover my ears, broken wrist and all. My teeth clenched against the pain, my lungs rapid-firing in and out.

And then it was gone, the tempest of light and sound disappearing as quickly it came.

I was still on my back. The hot, acrid smell of burned silk and rubber invaded my nostrils. The foot that was about to kick me was frozen in backswing. It hung where it was for another tick before falling away. All around me, severed legs fell like bowling pins.

Again, I tried to lift myself from the ground, but I

barely budged. Somewhere in the distance, I heard the wail of an alarm. It didn't sound very loud to me, a sign the stims were wearing off. My eyes rolled up in my head, and my eyelids came slowly down, my heart soaring with the promise of sleep.

A voice shouted but I was already blissfully gone.

Until a slap struck my cheek.

I tried to protest, but only managed a grunt. Another slap made my eyes spring open. A woman was above me, her face hidden behind a complex pattern of inked numbers. The same woman from the metalworks shop.

She snatched my shirt and pulled me up. "We have to go!"

Pain seized my body, and I started to shake as I tried to get my good leg under me.

"Dammit," said the tattooed woman. "You can't walk."

No shit, was what I thought. What actually left my mouth must've sounded like a gurgle.

She hefted me up and somehow managed to balance my torso across her shoulders. Hugging my right arm and right leg, which were now dangling past her head, she started to trot as I bounced painfully along in her firefighter's carry.

The turf was littered with destruction. Chests blown open to reveal twisted wreckages of carbon fiber and neoceramics. A severed head had landed near a lamppost, its forehead severely dented, eyes darker than the night sky beyond the dome. Arms with mangled frames were scattered across the landscape as far as fifty feet. Hydraulic fluids leaked out onto the grass.

I saw flashlights near one of the exits. Managing to move my pinky, I gave my savior a couple warning taps. *They're coming.* With a grunt, she picked up her pace. For once, I was happy I hadn't been eating much the last six months, the weight I'd shed definitely made me a lighter load.

We reached the koi pond. Its dreamlike surface barely rippled in the lamplight. If she moved fast, she might get us out through the same exit I'd avoided earlier. Navya might still be waiting there.

But the tattooed woman didn't turn to stay out of the lamplight like I expected. Instead, she trudged straight for the pond. I tapped with my pinky again in some vain attempt to inform her we were about to fall in.

Her feet went into the water, but there was no splash or spray. I tried to understand how that could be possible as she marched forward.

I looked at her feet but had to blink my eyes clear to be sure of what I was seeing. The water had parted around her legs like a pond-sized version of the Red Sea. Already two feet deep, she went slowly to keep from slipping on the muddy surface. She went deeper, walls of water surrounding her hips while curious koi looked on.

Finally, I managed to speak, but the only words I could get out were, "What the hell?"

She dropped me down onto the mud and kicked a

hatch that lay on the bottom of the pond. She kicked again, using her heel to signal somebody below. The hatch might have seemed strange if I wasn't so fascinated by the gravity-defying walls of water that surrounded us. I'd never seen an antigravity device work on such a small scale or with such precision.

What was that weapon she used? How could she take out thirteen botsies with a single shot? And come to think of it, where the hell did she come from?

She kicked the hatch with the heel of her boot one last time, the resulting clang making my head hurt even more than it did already. I looked at my bad leg, noticing for the first time that a piece of bone jutted through my pant leg. Suddenly nauseous, I began to gag, the wracking motion setting my ribcage on fire.

The hatch handle clanked open and somebody pushed it up from below.

A head rose from the hole, his eyes instantly landing on me. First on my face, then my badly butchered ankle. "Hand her to me," he said.

"She's too heavy for you," she said. "Get out of my way."

"Give her to me," he insisted, his tone firm enough to snuff any kind of argument.

Voices sounded from somewhere behind me. Whoever was coming, they were getting close.

The woman snatched my good arm and yanked me toward the hatch. I slid through the mud, hugging my bad wrist to my chest as the first part of me dropped into the hole.

He caught me with firm hands, his grip tight and comforting as he lowered me to the floor of a crawl space. He struggled to pull me toward a bigger tunnel bathed in bright light. The tattooed woman dropped through and slammed the hatch closed behind her, and I thought I heard the clap of water as the pond above collapsed upon itself.

She was helping now, the two of them pulling me out of this low-ceilinged alcove. Into the tunnel, they hefted me up onto the back of a motorized cart. He stayed with me while the woman nabbed the wheel and stomped the accelerator.

He touched my cheek. "Don't worry," he said. "I'm going to get you fixed up."

My eyes closed, the last thread of consciousness starting to slip though my fingers.

"*Arigato*, Ojiisan."

CHAPTER SIXTEEN

HE WAS THERE WHEN I WOKE UP. MY grandfather. The man who sat by my bed when I was sick as a child. And he was here now, sitting in a chair, legs crossed, glasses resting low on his nose.

"Welcome back," he said.

The room was large, a high ceiling towering far above. Light angled down through wooden rafters. The walls were made of banded stone. Every few feet, a water spout came from the wall, all of them pleasantly trickling into a brook that meandered the room. His chair and my cot were on a small island connected to the outer area by a high-arched bridge.

I rubbed my eyes, not noticing for a moment that my broken wrist was functioning without pain.

Seeing the surprise on my face as I stared at my bandage, Ojiisan said, "See, I told you I'd get you patched up."

A small filament hung out from under the bandages.

"It's a shunt," he said. "It looks like a thread, but it's actually a very narrow tube for deploying the nanobots."

I pulled the blanket up to expose my ankles and lifted my left leg. Again, I saw bandages and another shunt but felt no pain other than a little soreness as I rotated my foot. Reaching under the blanket, I touched my kneecap. Through the bandage, it felt whole beneath my fingers. Lastly, I filled my lungs as far as they would go, feeling little more than a faint ache in my chest.

"How long have I been out?"

"Four days. It's safest to keep you under as the bots do their thing. The physician is coming in a few hours to give you a checkup. If all goes as expected, he says it will only be one more day before you can resume normal activity. Until then, no strenuous movements. Oh, and since he's coming close to dinner, I invited him to stay and dine with us."

"Where's Smith?"

"He's fine. You're safe here. My security systems are the best on Mars, so I left your gun upstairs. I didn't think you'd need it."

<Smith?>

<I'm here, Denver. I'm upstairs just like he said.>

<Are you okay?>

<Yes. Some of my memory modules were jarred loose from the impact of that kick, but your grandfather managed to fix them. One of his people was able to find

me lodged in the branches of the hedge maze. By the way, I've tapped into the security systems for this building, and like he says, they're top notch. I don't think Rafe can get to you as long as you're here.>

I scanned the room some more. Though it was impossible, the rock walls looked totally natural, like this space had been hollowed by winds. "Where are we?"

"Like it? It's yours, you know."

I sat up on my cot. The floor underneath was tiled with broad stone rectangles. To my right was a rock garden, a soothing pattern of lines raked into the gravel around several isles of precisely arranged stones.

"You live here?"

"I live upstairs. I know it doesn't look like it, but we're actually on the tenth floor. Floors ten through twelve are ours. I bought the space a few months ago."

"It's amazing. I thought you'd lost it all twenty years ago. You know, when you were dead. How many other assets did you keep hidden?" I held back from saying the last two words, *from me*.

"A few," he said. "But they're all yours. If you hadn't saved me, I'd arranged for them all to be willed to you in two more years. Everything I have is yours when I'm gone. If you want some of it now, we can talk about that." He put his hand over his heart like he was making a promise. "No strings. I swear."

He pointed at a bare patch of flooring beyond the brook. "I plan to add some trees over there. I have a small greenhouse where I'm growing a few dozen junipers and maples from seeds. I've already started wiring some of the limbs."

"Shaping as they grow," I said.

"The key is to see the shape that pleases you and accentuate it. Trees are not clay. You can't just create any form you want. You have to see the tree first. See what it aspires to be and help it reach its potential."

I nodded. It was a lesson he'd taught me before.

He leaned in my direction. "That was what I tried to do with you, you know."

"You think I'm a tree?"

He smiled. "You are far more beautiful of mind and spirit than any tree. Maybe a little more stubborn, too," he winked. "But the rest of the metaphor holds true. I'm proud of you. Proud of who you've become."

I gave him a disbelieving stare. If there was one word that shouldn't be used to refer to me, that was it. I was a bad friend to Navya. A worse girlfriend to Vic, who wised up and took off months ago. My business's finances were held together by duct tape and wishful thinking. When I wasn't working, I was just a low-rent junkie. I was nothing to be proud of.

Looking at this man who raised me, knowing how he sold his people out, I couldn't even be proud of my lineage.

He said, "Don't dismiss my words so fast, little one. I know your life isn't everything you hoped it would be, and I take the blame for all of it, but your roots and limbs are strong. It's only a matter of time before you fully flower."

"Again with the bonsai metaphor?"

"Did I push it too far?" He smiled. "Perhaps so, but I want you to understand that you're far more centered than you think. I put you in an unwinnable situation after you rescued me and gave me my memories back. Yet, you found a way. It wasn't my way. Or Hennessey's way. It was your way."

"I did what was best for Mars."

He let out a small sigh. "Indeed, you did."

"Who was that woman? The one with the tattoos on her face?"

"Her name is Ace."

"She's one of them, isn't she?"

"I don't know much more than her name. What makes you think she's an alien?"

"A hunch. Whatever she used to stop Rafe's botsies, I've never seen anything like it. And she could move water like Moses. But I can't see it in her eyes like the others. If she is a bug, she's different."

"I think you're right," he said. "They walk among us. I've never found a way to tell them apart from humans. Some you can kind of tell, but that's only the incredibly bizarre and awkward ones like Doctor Werner. Others, though, are perfectly socialized. Ace seems like a good example of the latter except for the ink all over her face. All I know about her is she's new to Mars."

"How new?"

"She arrived just six days ago. She came from the belts, or at least that's what her papers said when she presented them to customs."

Smith was right. The numbers on her face were coordinates that pointed to the stars.

"How do you know her?"

"I don't, but she came to me. She told me you were in danger, and she was right."

"Are you telling me I have an alien for a guardian angel?"

He shrugged. "You should eat," he said before punching something up on his tablet. "Would that be so bad having a guardian angel? Whoever she is, she saved your life."

"What are they called?"

"The shapeshifters? As far as I know, they don't have a name."

"How is that possible? Everybody has a name."

"I asked Werner himself a long, long time ago, and that's what he told me. There's a lot I don't know about them."

"You knew enough to sign our future away to them."

His lips pinched ever so slightly at the dig. "Like you, I did what I thought was best for Mars. I got us the best bargain I could. You got a nice little introduction to their technology in the Earth Park. I've seen much, much worse. Trust me, when I say their bag of tricks doesn't have a bottom."

"How would you know? You don't even know their name?"

A man appeared from around a corner. He carried a tray topped by a bowl and a large glass of water. My grandfather and I watched silently as he delivered the soup—miso—and went back out the way he came.

Gods, it smelled good. The first spoonful didn't disappoint, and I had to restrain myself from slurping straight from the bowl.

"The food on Mars is so much better than when we started here," said Ojiisan. "So much more like home. I wish you could've seen Hiroshima before Earth got so bad. It was such a beautiful place when I was young."

I attacked my glass of water with the same enthusiasm as my soup, sucking down half the glass with my first gulp. "Can I talk to this Ace? I have questions for her."

"I knew you would. I invited her to dinner, too."

CHAPTER SEVENTEEN

I SIPPED A RED WINE, FEELING GUILTY FOR enjoying it while Nigel was still in Rafe's hands, while the job Jard hired me for remained unfinished, while the poor families who had lost their loved ones to that atrocity of a lab still had no closure. I'd checked the news. Those people, at least the ones with known identities, were still listed as missing.

The kitchen was far bigger than my apartment. Tall windows looked out upon a group of new buildings nestled under a vast dome. I'd never been to this part of Mars City before. According to my grandfather, construction had recently been completed.

Between the buildings was open space of craggy rock and small dunes. The builders had wisely preserved much of the natural desolation of the Martian landscape, except they'd added running paths and a pair of oases surrounded by synthetic palm trees and cacti. Protected by the dome, there were no sandstorms here. Beyond the peaceful tranquility of the dome though, I knew constant maelstroms raged. Not a bad metaphor for how I felt at the moment, back under the calming wing of the only parent I ever really knew.

A few people wandered about outside, some in running gear, others in swimsuits. Evidently there must have been a pool out there, though I couldn't see it from my vantage point. A pool.

This place was reserved for the richest of the rich, of which I was one if I could trust what my grandfather told me. I wasn't sure how I felt about that. On the one hand, I felt compelled to reject his entire legacy. On the other, I knew his wealth was borne of hard work and incredible risk. Despite all of the problems I had with my grandfather, what he and Hennessey had done in founding Mars Colony was an accomplishment I couldn't deny.

A bell rang. "I'll get it," I said to Ojiisan, who was working over the stove.

I headed toward the foyer.

<Smith, tap the cam feed. Can you see who it is?> I said.

<Yes, and you aren't going to like who's on the other side of that door.>

I stopped. <Is it safe?>

<I hope so…>

I went to the foyer and stepped up to the stone

door. Somehow, the massive slab of granite had been so perfectly balanced, it took hardly a tug to pull it open.

Ace stood in the corridor, but she hadn't come alone. To her left was Doctor Werner, a slithery smile on his face. Despite the shock, I managed to stutter out a hello.

My grandfather appeared behind my shoulder. "Welcome!" he called like he was greeting great friends. "So glad you could make it. You both know Denver," he said.

"We do," said Ace.

I tried to smile. Tried to say something...anything... but seeing Doctor Werner had knocked me totally off guard. This was the man who wanted to enslave us. The man who created red fever. The monster who sponsored that disgusting lab. Finally, I managed to find my voice. "Doctor, I wasn't expecting you."

"Nonsense," said Ojiisan. "I told you he was coming."

"You did?" I asked with a slightly embarrassed shake of my head. "Sorry, I might not be as recovered from my injuries as I thought. When you said the physician was coming, I thought you meant my doctor."

"He is your doctor," said Ojiisan.

My head snapped in the direction of my grandfather. "You let him touch me?"

"I let him heal your injuries, if that's what you're asking. His kind knows more about the human body than any of our finest doctors. How else could they take our form so easily?"

Ojiisan took me by the elbow before I could protest further and led me into the dining room, the two guests trailing behind.

The table had been set, probably by the servant who brought me my soup. I saw no sign of him now, though. Considering the sensitive nature of the talks that were sure to happen tonight, my grandfather must've dismissed him for the day.

Ojiisan went around the table filling wine glasses as the rest of us sat down, me across from Ace. My fingers twitched as they hung where Smith normally rode my hip. Though I knew I was in no danger, I still craved the peace of mind he brought to my increasingly fragile mind.

"Now," said Ojiisan, "I appreciate you all coming tonight. Dinner is ready, and it promises to be quite tasty, but I think it's best to keep it warm until we've had time clear the air."

The doctor sipped his wine and smacked his lips. His hair was greasy and uncombed. Magnified eyes stared out from behind thick eyeglasses. Ace picked up her glass and held it to the light. Next, she gave it a long sniff like some kind of connoisseur. She brought the glass to her lips and took a very tentative sip. Her eyebrows rose like she was surprised by the taste.

"It's called wine," I said. "Fermented juice from fruit called grapes."

"It's...interesting," she said. "Better than that beer so many of you seem to like."

"Where did you come from?"

"The belts," she said with a foxlike grin. "Just like it says on my papers."

"And your face."

She gave me a surprised look.

"I know what you are," I said.

"Sounds like you're quite the detective," she said with a heavy note of sarcasm. "Your reputation doesn't disappoint."

I was about to snap back but my grandfather cut me off. "Let's keep this civil, shall we? Denver, maybe you should thank Ace for saving your life?"

My gut felt tight at the thought of extending her—a bug—any kindness. But what was right was right. "I wouldn't have survived without your help. Though you don't owe me anything, I hope you'll tell me why you saved me."

She turned her head to look at Doctor Werner. "Ask him," she said.

He licked his lips. "She was following my orders. So, you should be thanking me as well."

I shook my head. I didn't know her well enough to hate. But this bastard would get no thanks from me. Ever.

"Glad to see you're up and about," he said.

"You have some nerve," I said. "You take people and

use them as lab rats and you think you can just wash that all away by sending her to save me?"

"As long as we're talking about ingratitude," he said, "you never thanked me for restoring your grandfather's memories. Without me, he'd still be a blank slate. His memories would forever be trapped in that gun of yours." He crossed his arms. "I know you think I'm a monster, but that doesn't give you an excuse to be rude."

I was too stunned to respond. He thought nothing of cutting our heads open, and he wanted politeness?

"Let's move on," said Ojiisan.

"We will not move on," said the doctor as he leaned forward and put his elbows on the table. "She owes me earnest thanks, and she owes me an apology for destroying my specimens."

My grandfather looked at me, a fatigued expression of concession on his face.

"You can't expect me to apologize," I said to him.

"Trust me," Ojiisan said. "We won't get very far until you make him happy."

"Happy?" I said, my voice rising. "Who cares about his happiness? He's an invader. An occupier. He's the goddamned enemy," I said with a bang of my fist on the table, surprised when I didn't feel pain in my wrist.

Chagrinned, my grandfather put his hands up in surrender. To the doctor, he said, "Maybe we should agree to disagree?"

The doctor rapped his fingers on the table, his

eyes boring into mine. "Would an enemy tend to your wounds? Would an enemy pay your bills?"

"What was that?"

"You heard me," he said with a cold grin. "I'm the one who hired you."

I felt a sick twinge in my gut. "The hell you say?"

"Is that any way to talk to a client?"

I knew my mouth was hanging open, but I made no attempt to close it. My mind scrambled to stay moored to the shifting ground.

"I hired you," he said. "When you were looking for all of those missing people, you were working for me."

"No." I shook my head. "My client was a family member of one of the missing."

"What's his name?" he asked. "What's her name? Or did your client request anonymity?"

<Smith, have you been listening to this?>

<Yes.>

<Is it true?>

<It could be.>

"Follow the money," said Doctor Werner. "And see if it takes you to account number three-four-seven-seven-zero-two..."

Before I could make the request, Smith said, <I'm running a trace on the payments right now. Looks like the funds passed through several accounts before it originated from source account three-four-seven-seven-zero-two—>

<That's enough,> I cut him off without letting finish the account number.

My head snapped in the direction of my grandfather. "I didn't know," he said. "Not until now."

I looked at Ace. She appeared to have no interest in what was going on. Half her wine was gone.

"You're a liar," I said to the doctor. "You expect me to believe you wanted me to find those missing people? The very people you yourself abducted?"

"I had nothing to do with those abductions," he said.

"The scientist in that lab was a shapeshifter. I blew his head apart myself, so don't tell me you had nothing to do with it."

"I didn't do it, Denver. You said it yourself. If I was in charge of that operation, then why would I hire you to stop it? The fact that I hired you proves it wasn't me."

I picked up my wine glass and took a big swig. What was hell was going on? How was I supposed to believe Werner was the good guy in this mess?

The doctor picked a piece of bread from the basket and cut himself a big slab of butter. "I brought Ace in to help the investigation, and help she did, no?"

"She did," I said.

"I would've left you out of it and hired her from the beginning, but she was two months away from Mars, and I didn't want to wait that long to start investigating the abductions. So, I hired you first."

"The belts are only three weeks away."

He grabbed the honey jar and, ignoring his spoon, he poured a puddle on his plate. “She came as quick as she could. She was passing through customs right about the same time you discovered that lab.” He dipped his bread and took a bite, a shiny smear of honey sticking to his thin lips.

“You cleaned up that lab. You got rid of the evidence.”

“Ace did that,” he said. “But it was under my orders. Only a very select few humans know about us, and I plan to keep it that way. Since I’m the only one who can terraform this world, you better plan to keep it that way.” He took another bite, a drop of honey now glistening on his stubbled chin.

I tossed my napkin over to him, but he left it where it was. “Now can we talk about our common problem, Mr. Rafe Ranchard?” he asked.

“No,” I said. “Not yet. First, tell me what was going on in that lab. Why did that shapeshifter have a human brain in his head?”

“Some grow impatient,” he said before taking another chomp of his bread.

“What does that mean?”

“They try to force the issue.”

“What issue is that?” I asked.

“Our attempts at human mind control are behind schedule.”

I waited for him to elaborate, a slight grin on my

face at hearing him admit failure even if it was barely an admission at all.

Then again, maybe it wasn't.

For the first time in months, I felt a little hope trickling into my consciousness. New possibilities bubbled up in my mind, and I decided to push them. "You can't do it, can you?"

"Nonsense." He swallowed down the last bite of bread and took a sip of his wine.

I was beaming now. Defiance felt so much better than defeat. "You can't control us," I laughed. "You've been trying to take over our minds for decades, and you've given up. You've tried every last thing you can think of, and it hasn't worked. That's why red fever is on the decline."

The doctor said nothing. Instead he went for another piece of bread. I looked at Ace, who now looked plenty interested in hearing the doctor's response. I turned to Ojiisan. He was staring at me, alert eyes seeming to say, *Could it be?*

"We're special," I said, almost not believing it as I spoke. How could humans be special? We'd destroyed our own planet. Soiled our own home like the basest of animals.

"Special?" asked the doctor. "I think not. Just different from the others."

"How many others are there? How many have you conquered and enslaved?"

"Hundreds," said Ace.

"How long does it usually take?" I asked. "A year? A month? A week?"

The doctor brushed the question away with a swipe of his hand. "I'm not here to talk about that. Can we get back to Rafe Ranchard?"

"Eager to change the subject, are we?" The sarcastic smirk on Ojiisan's face said my newfound confrontational attitude might be contagious.

Doctor Werner didn't make eye contact, his gaze now aimed at his bread. When he finally met my eyes, I savored the way the corners of his eyes were pinched like the chandelier was suddenly too bright, and the way his lips were drawn as if he'd just sucked a rotten lemon. His eyes quivered in their sockets, unable to focus on me or anybody else. Light reflected off of them like gemstones in a way only I could see. A way that professed his non-human origins. He adjusted the wrist-cuffs of his shirt as if he'd just realized it didn't fit right. I'd hit home alright. He knew he couldn't break us.

Hope washed over me. We still needed them to keep terraforming this world, but we didn't have to become their slaves. We could fight. We had a puncher's chance, and I was ready to throw some haymakers.

"The man who ran that lab," I said, "he was taking matters into his own hands because you, Doctor, are a failure. That's what you meant when you said some are impatient. He put a human brain in his own head to see if he could figure us out because he's been waiting twenty years for you to deliver, and you've got nothing."

He didn't respond, so I repeated myself. If I could've, I would've shouted it to the masses at the top of my lungs. "You are a total, complete failure."

The doctor barely blinked. Same for Ace, who seemed to be hanging on every word.

My grandfather looked like he was very much enjoying himself as he refilled his wine. Perhaps I'd been too hard on him. From the beginning, he was convinced we had less-than-zero chance of stopping them. Take away a man's hope, and his ideals were sure to follow.

Still, I might never be able to stomach the idea of him shaking that bug's hand. Understanding somebody's actions wasn't the same as forgiving them.

I turned back to Werner. "Tell me I'm wrong," I said, challenging him to get off the mat.

"Rafe Ranchard is a danger," he said, choosing to bull his way into a new topic. "I don't think any of us believe the Peerless Leader is really sick. Three of the bodies in that lab were Hennessey's loyalists."

"Three? I knew one was a priest."

"The other two were bishops. Rafe is sending the rest of the church a message. Comply with his takeover or disappear. He won't stop until the church is his."

I nodded unsurprised to discover yet another example of Rafe's ratfuckery. "So what if Rafe takes the church?" I asked.

He turned a puzzled eye on me. "I'd think you'd be terrified of him seizing more power. You and he are famously antagonistic toward each other."

"I know how I feel about Rafe. What I want to know is how you feel about him. What do you care who runs the church? Why aren't you celebrating Hennessey's fall? You and he are famously antagonistic toward each other."

He fidgeted in his seat. "My motives aren't any of your business. Do you agree that Bishop Ranchard needs to be stopped or not?"

"I do."

"Good. Then I'd like to hire you to assassinate him."

CHAPTER EIGHTEEN

I STOOD IN THE BASEMENT OF MY grandfather's building, waiting. Giant fan blades were barely visible through thick blankets of fibra-filter stained by layers of dust and grit. Behind the air filtration system was a hatch, much like the strange hatch that sat at the bottom of the pond Ace and I escaped through.

Both hatches led to a tunnel system, according to my grandfather. They were just two of dozens of similar hatches all around Mars City.

He left diggers behind before he was banished to live on the surface decades ago. Diggers that had been programmed to build a network of tunnels all his own. For twenty years, they'd drilled and burrowed, always careful to stay hidden as they constructed their mazy warren of passages.

An escape plan was what he told me. Should the day come that his deal with the aliens became public, he figured he'd need a safe place to hide until the aliens regained control of the mob. According to the map he'd shared with Smith, there were more than thirty safe rooms and bunkers stocked with supplies.

Yet another amazing surprise from the man who rose from the dead. I had a feeling it wouldn't be the last.

<What time is it?> I asked Smith, who was back where he belonged on my hip.

<It's time. She should be here any minute.>

Two days had passed since the dinner with Doctor Werner, and I still couldn't believe I'd agreed to his proposition. My heart raced at the thought of it.

I was going to assassinate Rafe Ranchard.

It was him or me, after all. As long as Rafe Ranchard was alive, I'd never, ever feel safe anywhere on this planet. I'd never escape the long and dangerous reach of his hooded shadow. Backed by an army of botsies, reinforced by the church's zealots and cultists, I was good as dead if I ever stepped out from the confines of my grandfather's high-security home.

As if I needed further convincing, Doctor Werner promised to pay incredibly well. So well, I could get Nigel fixed up, assuming I managed to recover him. I could even get his chip reprogrammed if Rafe tampered with any of his systems.

Kill Rafe, and I'd make good on the job Jard hired me to do. Kill him and I might even save Hennessey, who was still alive, according to the latest news reports.

Those same news reports were replete with images of Rafe glad-handing every single voting member of the church, no doubt securing their support to be the new Peerless Leader before putting Hennessey under for good. Save Hennessey, and Mars could reclaim the staunchest member of its resistance against the bugs.

So I took the job. How could I not? Mars couldn't fall into the hands of a madman. Now was a time for leadership and vision. Not the insane fanaticism of Rafe Ranchard.

The ethics of it all certainly stuck in my craw. If I was willing to take money to commit murder, then what was next on the slippery slope of moral decay?

But I'd done a lot of things recently I wasn't proud of. No matter how dirty the job made me feel, I clung to the fact that this was a mission of self-defense. A mission of rescue for both Hennessey and Nigel. Who was I to claim the moral high ground when the stakes were so high?

The door opened and Ace strode through with Ojiisan a safe distance behind. "Ready?" she asked.

I nodded.

She turned to my grandfather, who glanced at me before asking Ace to give us a minute.

"Hurry," she said and ducked back out the door.

"You're sure about this?" he asked.

I nodded. "Are you sure he'll be there?"

"He will," he said. "It's all in the church scripture. The passages on the promotion of a new Peerless Leader is very specific. *The Peerless Leader's last breath will be passed through the lips of the gods to a successor. It's your best chance to get Rafe alone.*"

"Good," I said. "Then we're all set. It will all be over before dinner."

Ojiisan dipped his head and sighed as he gathered his thoughts. "Denver," he said, his eyes misting over. "You don't know how much I've missed you these last months."

I didn't know what to say. That I'd missed him too? That I'd missed him the last twenty years?

"I know it's difficult for you to be here with me," he said. "I know you might never forgive me. I'm not sure I deserve to be forgiven, but I need you to know how much I love you."

A tear broke free from his eye.

He rested a hand on my shoulder. "First, I need you to stay safe, understand me? And second, I hope that after this is over, you'll be willing to visit sometime."

I fought against a suddenly quivering lip. "We'll see," I said.

He waited for me to say more, but when I didn't, he offered a gentle bow of understanding. He tried to smile, but the disappointment inside him was too great to let the smile blossom.

I didn't have any words to express the monsoon of emotions sweeping through me. The little girl in me wanted nothing more than to forgive and forget. To pull him into my arms and start making up for lost time.

But the adult in me was still too wounded. Too hurt.

"I have to go," I said.

He opened the door to let Ace back through, and then he left without another word.

Ace took one look at my face and went to wait by the filtration system. I wiped my eyes, frustrated by the cruelty of the situation. I didn't want to hurt the man who raised me, yet I did, and the guilt was tearing me up. I shook my head at how unfair it was. He was the one who'd done wrong, and I was the one standing here feeling guilty.

My eyes cleared, and I sniffled away the last of my emotions. I had a job to do.

Dropping to her stomach, Ace wormed into a narrow gap under the vent's grating. Wind whipped my head as I followed her to the floor to match her wriggling progress.

Reaching the hatch, Smith sent the signal to unseal the lock. A few awkward turns of the hatch wheel and Ace swung the door open to let us squirm through.

With barely enough room to stand upright, I kept my head low and raised Smith so he could light my way. "Did you remember to bring a lightbeam?" I asked Ace.

In response she snapped her fingers and brought a firefly into existence. That was what it looked like circling above her head, except it didn't blink on and off. Instead it bathed her in a soft glow that seemed to bring her face tattoos alive with an eerie phosphorescence. I reached for the light, but my hands passed right through it. Magic was the word that popped into my head, but I held back from saying it aloud. I didn't want to give her the satisfaction of flummoxing the primitive human with her little tricks, stunning as they were.

We started our march, and it would be a long one. "Ace," I said to her back. "Thanks for giving us a moment back there."

"Not a problem," she said. "Your people require substantial energy to process your emotions."

"You know, I can't help but notice, you're a lot more, um…socialized than Doctor Werner. How is it you could see to give us space when the doctor would've missed the signals?"

"We're not of the same type."

"What does that mean?"

She didn't answer. Maybe that was why I couldn't see the flicker in her eyes.

<Another hundred feet before the first turn,> said Smith. <Then go left.>

I'd spent plenty of time the last two days studying the tunnel map, but it was nearly impossible to read. Like trying to trace string that was knotted into a ball the size of a bolder. Lucky for me, I had an AI to map it out. I called out the turn and followed Ace as the tunnel sloped downward and started shading even further to the left.

"Why kill Rafe?" I wanted to know.

"I was hired to do the same job as you."

"But what's the doctor's motivation?"

She didn't respond to that one either.

"It's political, isn't it? He's got competition who thinks they can do a better job breaking our minds. He's afraid of losing his job."

"It's more than a job. It's a governorship."

"Governor of Mars? The solar system? All of humanity?"

Instead of answering, she started up a steep slope careful to follow the series of footholds.

"Do we matter to you?" I asked.

She stopped for a moment and examined the carved edges of the footholds in the rock.

"You and your people are tools. Much like the tools used to sculpt the path before us and the dwellings above us, you serve a purpose. And for now, you have value. But once your purpose has been served, you'll mean no more to me than the forgotten machines rusting away on the surface."

The next five hours were much of the same. Me asking lots of questions. Her throwing up one stone wall after another just like the maddening tangle of tunnels that seemed designed to disorient anybody who dared to enter.

My feet were sore. Same for my shoulders and neck from having to duck most of the way. My water and a small stash of protein paste I'd brought were empty. Keeping up with Ace wasn't easy. She moved effortlessly and relentlessly forward.

Our path moved downward. Slopes and stairs and ladders, all of them leading deeper and deeper into Mars' crust.

<Okay, Denver, there's a hatch dead ahead.>

Ace must've already spotted it, her pace hastening to reach our destination.

<I've disengaged the lock,> said Smith an instant before Ace began spinning the wheel. She pulled the handle, but it didn't budge. She lowered her balance and gave it another tug with no success. Soon we were both on the floor, our feet wedged against the wall, pulling hard enough that I thought the muscles in my back might snap like rubber bands.

<I think it's the air pressure,> said Smith. <Just have to break the seal. Get me close.>

I told Ace to stand back and held Smith inches from the hatch. A laser drilled into the steel, a tear of molten iron dripped down a second later. Unable to keep Smith perfectly level, the hole widened into a divot. After a few minutes of effort, the laser punched clear through.

Air whistled from the hole, a high-pitched whine that made me cover my ears as the air on either side of the hatch began to equalize. When the sound began to subside, I easily swung the door open while Ace watched with raised eyebrows. I tucked Smith back into my belt. Ace wasn't the only one who could make magic.

I ducked low. The air on the other side smelled fresh compared to the still air of my grandfather's tunnels.

I reached my hands through to the ledge on the other side of the opening, my fingers dropping into a shallow pool of water.

I crawled forward, the knees of my pants instantly soaked. I gathered my feet under me and stood up slow so I could take it all in. I'd never believed this place was real, but here it was, unfolding right before my eyes.

CHAPTER NINETEEN

FOR YEARS, RUMORS HAD SPREAD—SOME OF them whispers, some of them shouts—but none of them had ever been verified until now.

My grandfather wasn't the only one who had grabbed diggers for his own. Decades after Mars City was excavated, most of the vast fleet of equipment sat abandoned on the surface, a sprawling trash heap of hulking skeletons that were literally being eaten alive by the scouring power of the sandstorms.

But Hennessey, the co-founder of Mars, had taken some for himself. In fact, according to Ojiisan, an entire fleet of them, and at least a few of them were mega-diggers, not the detailers my grandfather had managed to coopt for his own purposes twenty years ago.

"Make room," said Ace.

I stepped to the side without looking away from the panorama stretched out before me.

Panorama. The very thought of it was practically foreign to anybody who grew up underground. But the view ahead was so vast, it seemed there was no limit. Even on Mars' surface, your eye couldn't reach so far. Whether it was jagged mountain peaks or craterous breaks in the surface, there was always an obstruction in the distance. Every schoolchild knew the planet's curvature would eventually tilt a landscape out of your view, but not in this place. It had no edge other than the one at my back.

Ojiisan hadn't been here himself, but Hennessey had shared the blueprints with him a long time ago. That was when the church was new. When they were still partners. Before they became bitter rivals.

The entire structure had been built underground, and it was perfectly level. To my left and right, it stretched flat as a laser beam as far as the eye could see. A vast plane, dug deep enough that it reached for kilometers without interruption.

The ceiling was high, maybe sixty feet tall, lifted by smooth, thick columns that stood like a forest of redwoods topped by arches gnarled and textured to mimic limbs and branches. Every column had lights attached near the ceiling, all blossoming with a soothing glow that made this cavern of unforgiving stone seem soft and warm.

Cool liquid soaked the sock on my left foot. Evidently my boots weren't watertight. The two inches of water on the floor sat so perfectly still it could be mistaken for glass. Snared in its limitless lens was an ethereal array of reflections that filled me with a rare sense of peace.

Helluva place for an assassination.

We started marching anew. It was two kilometers to the center, to the only spot that was dry. The place where you could sit on a large stone and meditate.

That was what this place was. The Peerless Leader's meditation chamber.

<I've been counting your steps. I think you're about halfway there,> said Smith. <But I can't say for sure since there's no map.>

The fact that the Peerless Leader had a meditation chamber was no secret. This was where he claimed—after months of reflection—to have conquered the feve. But other than Hennessey, nobody had ever been here. Everything about the chamber's size and location was a church secret, which meant Smith had no data on this place. The best he could do was estimate.

But we knew Rafe was here. The announcement from the church had gone up thirty minutes ago, just like Ojiisan predicted. Scripture was clear on the subject of succession, he'd explained. *The Peerless Leader's last breath will be passed through the lips of the gods to a successor.*

In other words, Hennessey was about to get snuffed, and when the doctors verified his last breath, Rafe would be in this chamber, receiving the blessing.

Prophecy would be complete. The church would be Rafe's.

My grandfather might've been missing his memories for twenty years, but now that he had them back, he knew more about Mars than I could ever hope to know.

Ace and I kept a cautious pace. We were in no rush. Rafe would be meditating for hours, maybe days, asking the gods for guidance. Asking for their approval. Asking for their direction.

Asking for a whole lot of bullshit if you asked me.

I kept marching, every step taking me closer to my objective. Creating a world where a scheming piece of garbage like Rafe Ranchard wouldn't gain power. A world where the aliens were so consumed with infighting, they could be divided further and vanquished.

What I wanted was a world where Nigel could live free.

A world where I had a purpose. A mission.

A world with hope.

Ace walked alongside me as a partner. Weapons hung from her belt. What they were capable of I couldn't guess, but I'd seen enough in the Earth Park to fill me with confidence. The water at my feet would soon run with Rafe's blood and there was nothing he could do to stop it. Released from whatever his insane vision was for Mars, I could refocus on our real enemy: the mercenary walking beside me and the doctor who brought her here.

The time passed quickly, Smith counting down every

kilometer in my head. I carried him in my fist now. <This is it, old friend. Mars is setting a new course.>

<It's good to have you back, Denver.>

Yes, it was. My heart was hammering with anticipation. I was taking back my life, and it felt so damn sweet. I could hardly believe the dark, depressed space I'd been in just a few days ago. It was as if that was a different person. A stranger who looked like me and sounded like me, but wasn't me.

<It's time to slow down,> said Smith. <According to my scans, I think you're getting very close to the center of this space.>

I gave Ace a hand signal, and we both dropped our pace, moving from column to column to stay in the shadows as much as possible.

<We're too deep for any kind of signal, Denver. I can't call for help so be very careful.>

The lighting was different ahead. Kilometers of uniformly placed columns had finally broken into a different pattern. They now stood closer together, and instead of being lined up as the ranks of an army, they were arranged in wide concentric circles, at the center of which I could barely make out a solitary seated figure.

Rafe.

My pulse raced at the sight of him. Our never-ending feud was about to run out of rope. It ended here. It ended now.

"Can you hit him from here?" whispered Ace.

<No, he’s barely a speck. Way too far for a handheld,> said the voice in my mind.

I shook my head. “You?”

“No. What is that over his head?”

I’d been so focused on our target, I hadn’t noticed, but now that I did, I had no idea what it was hovering in the air a few feet above where Rafe meditated. From this distance, it was just a white smear. Smith projected a magnified image in my mind, but I still couldn’t make it out. Wafts of smoke and steam rose from the ground and distorted the view. Whatever it was, it seemed to sway ever so slightly.

<Is that a person?>

<It could be, but I can’t make out the triangle shape protruding from the back. From here it almost looks like a dorsal fin.>

“We need to get closer,” I whispered. “Ace, can you do your water trick so we don’t make splashing noises?”

She pushed a button on one of the devices on her belt, and a narrow channel opened around her boots. “You’ll have to stay close.”

We walked single file, taking it slow to keep our heels from echoing too loudly on the stone. She led us laterally until our view of Rafe and whatever was suspended in the air above him were blocked by a line of columns. If we couldn’t see Rafe, he couldn’t see us.

Steadily, we crept closer and closer. Occasionally, when we had to circle a column, I caught a glimpse of

Rafe. He appeared to have shed his robes, his bare skin warm with the glow of a hundred candles circling his perch.

The thing hovering above him was clearer now. I could see for sure that it was indeed a person, but who it was, or how it managed to float in the air was still a mystery.

The smell of incense grew thicker with every step. I rubbed my nose to keep from sneezing as each column passed seemed to loom larger and larger.

Rafe stood. Ace and I froze. He didn't turn our way though. Instead, he used a pair of tongs to reach into a steel bin sitting atop a pile of hot coals. Lifting out a stone, he dropped it into a bucket of water that kicked up a cloud of hot steam. He leaned over it, letting it wash over him.

Slowly, tentatively, Ace and I started moving again. Finally, there was only one column between us and Rafe, both of us pressing our backs against the cool pillar.

<Ready, Smith?>

<As I'll ever be.>

Ace and I locked eyes. I held up a fist with three fingers, and started the countdown. The weapon in Ace's hand was like nothing I'd ever seen. A cylinder—not unlike the baton of a relay race—left me wondering if she was going to throw it like a stick of dynamite or shoot it like a mini bazooka.

I dropped my final finger. I gave Ace one last nod, then only managed one step before it all went to hell.

Ace was hit. Not by weapon fire, but by a fist. She dropped instantly, her face caved in like a crushed can. I brought Smith around, but didn't make it halfway before a bare foot slammed my wrist against the column. I cried out in pain, and Smith dropped from limp fingers.

I fell backward, into the water. He kicked me, my hip catching the worst before I hydroplaned across the floor, every inch of me instantly soaked.

I rolled face-up just in time to see him spring like a tiger. Water sprayed from his feet as he impossibly covered five, now ten, now twenty feet in the air. Another kick, this one catching me in the shoulder, sent me spinning like a top. Water got into my lungs and I was choking, desperate for air.

He was on top of me, the back of my head smacking hard against the stone floor. His fist clenching my throat.

I tried to push his arm away, but it was strong like rebar. I tried to buck him off but the legs straddling me were unmovable as bridge supports. I clawed at his elbow and wrist, my nails unable to dig into his skin.

I was fading fast, but I saw seams below his chin, a slight tone shift between the skin above and below the patch job.

Rafe was a botsie now. He'd replaced everything except for his head and face, which was bright with fury.

He pushed harder and what little oxygen was still wheezing down my windpipe strangled away.

CHAPTER TWENTY

I COULDN'T BREATHE. MY THROAT WAS collapsing. My consciousness hung by the thinnest of threads.

<Stay low,> said a voice in my mind. As if I could do anything else.

Water struck first. Like a thousand needles, it pelted my left side, every inch of it that was raised above the water level. Next came the pulse, which washed over me like a tsunami.

Rafe went with it. All of him but one arm, which still clutched my throat.

Coughing and sputtering, I gathered enough strength to wrench the hand's grip off my throat.

<I got him, Denver. I used the same trick I used in the lab to line up a shot.>

<Gods, I love you, Smith.> And I meant it. I'd never

loved him more. I wished all relationships could be as easy.

I managed to stand. My left shoulder was on fire, but I could still move my arm. My hip hurt like hell too, but it functioned. Rafe's body lay face down in the water. Swirls of fluids spread from gaping wounds. Seams of skin were visible at the joints.

I turned his head with the heel of my boot, exposing the dead eye on the left side of his still face. Even dead, his expression was trapped in a mean sneer. Bending low, I clawed his cheek with my fingernails then leaned close to watch for blood. None came. Synthskin. Despite my earlier assessment, even his head was botsie.

A replica? Could the real Rafe still be hiding around here somewhere? No, I didn't think so. The last few times I'd seen him, he wore his robes long, so long that every inch of his body was covered. He had swapped out every piece of himself, and he didn't want anybody to notice the transformation.

I had to assume everything but the brain had been replaced. Replace the brain and he wouldn't be Rafe anymore. Memories could be copied, some of the personality too, but I knew better than most that didn't make Smith my grandfather. But how could a human brain be joined to a botsie body?

The bastard got alien help. The alien in that lab was trying to transplant human brains into bug bodies.

Interfacing a human brain with a botsie body was probably easy by comparison.

I shook my head, hardly believing it myself. Rafe was so in love with botsies, he decided to become one. And I bet the alien help he'd received to transition into a next generation android was his payment for providing that horrorshow of a lab.

I stood and looked over my shoulder at the floating form. It was Hennessey. He was suspended by rusty wires that had been run through his shoulder blades. Hanging like dead weight, the skin had stretched like the top of a circus tent. The fin, as Smith had called it.

I stepped closer. Ribs protruded from a withered torso, and I watched for any sign of breathing.

<Denver, he's still alive.>

<Yes, I think I see his chest moving. Barely.>

<No, not him. Rafe.>

I spun fast. Rafe was on his knees and he wobbled himself upright. One shoulder was completely missing, but somehow his broken legs were working. Same for his other arm. His head hung at an awkward angle, but he shoved it back into place with the palm of his hand.

Smith's voice cranked to maximum volume in my mind. <Run!>

Water kicked up with every footfall.

I glanced back. Rafe was running in my direction, but he was slowed by a bad hitch in his stride. I passed a column. Then another one.

I took a quick glance back. He was flying now, the hitch totally eliminated, his pace so perfect he seemed to glide across the water while my own steps kicked splashes high enough that water dotted my cheeks.

My right toe caught on something. With the realization I was going down, a sickening dread took hold. I hit the floor, the water barely cushioning the blow before I was skidding out of control. I scrambled to my feet as Rafe leapt over a prone form on the floor. It was Ace I'd tripped over.

I was sprinting again, picking up as much speed as I could, but it wouldn't be enough. He tackled me with one arm, his hold around my waist strong enough to squeeze the wind out of me. I was kicking and punching even before the tumble was complete, but all he needed was one quick shot to my jaw to put me under.

CHAPTER TWENTY-ONE

MY HEAD HURT. SAME FOR EVERY OTHER PART of me, yet one particular pain sung more loudly than the rest, the one from my back, specifically the area all around my shoulder blades.

I pried my eyes open. Jesus, not again.

I was in the air.

Hanging.

Hennessey was on the floor, and I knew I'd taken his place. My shirt had been ripped off, and I could feel the wires running through the stretched flesh in my back. I tried to scream, but my voice was too weak to do anything but grunt.

Wrenching my neck as far around as I could, I saw the apparatus that lifted me. The cable ran to a lever on the floor, which was, unsurprisingly, several feet out of reach.

<Smith?>

<I'm here, Denver.>

<Help me.>

<I can't. I've been dropped inside the bin full of hot rocks near the circle of candles. I can't shoot my way out, and we're way too deep to get a signal and call for help.>

I groaned as the last bit of hope drained out of me.

"I'm sorry, Denver," said a voice that was out of sight. "I didn't want to do this."

"Let me down," I said, tears welling in my eyes. "You win. Just let me down, R—" I stopped myself from finishing the name Rafe. The voice that spoke to me, it wasn't Rafe's. Nor was it that sad heap on the floor who once co-founded Mars Colony. The voice had a British accent.

A hand landed on my pantleg, and I was slowly spun around.

"Nigel?"

He nodded. "I couldn't stop him from reprogramming me. I have to follow his orders, but I used clean wire to string you up."

"Where is he?"

"Not far. He's torturing the alien. I didn't want him to touch my programming. I would've fought him, Denver. But I couldn't. I didn't have—"

"A body," I interrupted, my lip quivering. "I know. I never should've asked you to work undercover. It's my fault."

He lowered his head, and I thought I saw a blush in his cheeks. When he spoke, his voice was just a whisper. "I'm the one who did this to you. Me. I should've stayed with Jard. I can't be trusted with freedom. None of us can."

I shook my head. "You didn't do this. Rafe did."

Nigel turned his gaze away.

I wanted to argue some more. To tell him it would all be okay. He had a new body now, and we could fix his programming. We hadn't lost yet.

But we had. He was Rafe's. And so was I. Trapped. Pinned like a bug in a museum display. I kicked my legs and swung my arms, a scream welling up from deep within.

Nigel waited for my panicked fit to run out of steam before speaking again. "I did as tight a weave as I could with the length of wire I had," said Nigel. "I know that means I put more holes in your skin, but I thought it would reduce the pain to spread your weight across as many connection points as possible."

"You did good," I said, a tear dripping off my nose to fall in the water below. "You did good."

The sounds of splashing made me turn my head. Rafe was approaching. One-armed, he dragged Ace behind him like she was a kill from a hunting trip. He pulled her up next to Hennessey's unconscious form and released his grip on her ankle.

She was hurt. Legs and arms were badly twisted from multiple dislocations and breaks. I had little doubt I'd be in similar shape soon.

"Denver," said a naked Rafe. His botsie body was as

broad as his old one. A barrel chest was lined with seams of synthskin. His legs were thick as posts, and his right arm was missing. A deep gouge cut through his shoulder to expose wires and circuit boards, and his off-kilter head seemed like it was barely attached. How he was functioning was beyond me.

"So good of you," he said, "to hang out and wait for me." If that was a joke, he made no indication that he found himself funny. Instead, his face was its usual brash mask marked by a severe chin under tight lips and cruel eyes. His mechanical face was a perfect match for its biological inspiration. Botsies were always an amazing feat of technology, but Rafe's new form was no doubt a generational leap forward. "It's Hennessey's, you know."

"What is?"

"This device you're strung up on. Hennessey designed it for his own meditation when he fought the feve. He thought the pain it caused could drive the mind into another state. Meditation is a powerful force. I really believe that, but this device never made sense to me. Still, I figure I'll spend another day or two in here meditating the old-fashioned way. It's time to talk to the gods, time to receive their blessing."

"You're such a fraud," I said through clenched teeth. "To seize power, you killed two bishops and a priest, not to mention whatever poison you've been injecting into Hennessey. No god will bless you."

"The gods bless the winner, no matter what he had

to do to get there. As far as I'm concerned, the gods have already spoken, which is why I'm standing upright instead of lying like a heap of trash on the floor." He pointed at Hennessey's limp form.

"Still, I'll keep Mars in suspense for a time. Let them think the gods have lots to tell me. The transfer of power should be ceremonious, don't you think? Can't rush it or it will lose all its weight and gravitas. After all, it won't ever happen again."

"You plan to live forever?"

"Without the burden of a frail human body, there's no reason the brain can't live in perpetuity. I'm the next step in human evolution. The final step."

I closed my eyes against a ripple of pain seizing the pierced muscles in my back. "Final step? What are you talking about?"

"I'm the only one. I'll always be the only one. The perfect blend of the biological and the artificial. A sublime representation of our past and our future. Where once we were weak—" he kicked Hennessey, sending him sliding across the watery floor,"—now I am strong."

"Even the shapeshifters are stronger than humans," he said, pointing at Ace. "She looks hopelessly broken, but she's not. She's fixing herself as we speak."

"We're not weak," I said. "The aliens can't master us like so many other races. We're special."

"Only because they sent the bumbling Doctor Werner to unzip our minds." He pointed at Ace again.

"I've just confirmed what I've suspected all along. Werner was a political appointment. He doesn't know a lick about science."

"His terraforming efforts are pretty successful so far."

"That's child's play for them. The real challenge is bringing a species like ours to heel, and on that score, he's out of his league. But there are others on Mars right now. According to Ace, there are four of them who are more accomplished than the doctor when it comes to such things, and now I know their names. These other four are all vastly more talented than Doctor Werner. Like Bat, you remember him, don't you? He's the one who guided my evolution in exchange for giving him specimens and space to work. His research was promising. He only needed another month or two." He tapped my skull with a heavy finger. "He would've cracked your head like an egg if you hadn't killed him."

"Bullshit. We're different."

"You weary me, Denver, but let me indulge you for a second. Let's say you're right and their mind control never works. Don't you realize they can just choose to exterminate humanity instead? They can do it in the blink of an eye."

"Then why haven't they?"

"For now, they prefer to add humans to their already impressive list of subspecies. According to Ace, there's a galactic council out there somewhere, and the more species you control, the higher your status. We're just one of thousands of so-called intelligent organisms, and yet you're so arrogant to count us special? It's time you faced facts. Humans are an accident. A hopelessly feeble, flawed and self-destructive race of weaklings, though I grant you're stronger than most, Denver."

"No," I insisted. "We're stronger than you think."

He rubbed his jaw. "You've been a worthy adversary these last few years. Can I tell you a story? I've never told it to anybody, but I think you'll find it germane."

"D-do I have a choice?" I stuttered as my jaw began to quiver.

"No," he said. "I suppose not. You know my mother was a sandworm?"

My whole body started to shake. I was going into shock.

"Stay with me, now," he said before reaching to the floor to splash me with water. "A sandworm, you know the folks who used to live in tents and haul sand for the concrete used to build so much of our city. We were nomads, my brother and I tailing along behind my mother to whichever quarry was paying the most. You know what a sandworm's biggest fear is?"

He splashed me some more. "A sandworm's biggest fear, what is it, Denver?"

"L-losing c-containment," I said.

"That's exactly right. You're younger than I am. You grew up in the city, so you never had to worry about your air supply. Imagine being a child, constantly separated from your mother for shifts that ran twenty hours at a time. Hour after hour, it's just you and your brother sitting inside a dungeon of cloth with death waiting for you outside. Day after day, you know that the slightest tear in that fabric will suffocate you. You're afraid to touch the walls. Irrationally, you're afraid to let your fingernails grow too long. You're afraid to roughhouse like a growing boy should. And every little burp or cough of the air pump sends you into a panic, your heart galloping as beads of sweat gather on your brow. Can you picture what that must've been like?"

I nodded.

"Now imagine jerking awake in the middle of the night with a pillow over your face. 'It's a drill' says your brother. You have to practice. Have to see how long you can go without air. Without passing out or dying."

He splashed me some more, and the shakes started to fade, a creeping nausea taking its place.

"The drills go on for years," he said. "Sometimes just once in a week. Other times it happens several times the same night. After hundreds of these air drills, you'd think you'd get used to it. You'd think you'd learn to stay calm, but hard as you try, there's always a moment of sheer, uncontrollable panic. A moment where you try to squirm out from under that pillow. A moment where you try to kick and scratch your way out.

"That's the moment, Denver, that hateful, shameful moment when you cease to be strong. It's the moment when you succumb to being a victim. A goddamned victim. You try and try, but it gets the best of you every single time. You cry to your brother, and to your mother, beg for it to stop. You try to stay awake, poking yourself with a pin whenever you feel you're about to fall under, but none of it works. You keep falling asleep, and the drills keep coming, over and over and over."

"Y-you exp-pect me to f-feel sorry for you?"

"Of course not," he smiled. "I was the one holding the pillow. My brother, he just wouldn't learn."

All I could do was shake my head and hope the pillow would be coming for me sooner rather than later.

"He was weak," said Rafe. "He acted like I was just being mean, like I wasn't doing it for his own good. But losing containment is no joke. Once, I even punched a hole in our tent to show him how serious it was, but he got so hysterical, he passed out before getting his mask on. After another few months of utter failure, I realized he was too big of a disgrace to continue. One night, I just left the pillow in place."

I found my voice. "You're sick. Disgusting."

"He needed to be put down. He'd become a sad shell of himself. Just like the rest of humanity has. The whole human race is ready to be put down, don't you think? We lived as gods once. We built shining cities of glass and steel. Our artists and writers and filmmakers created remarkable works. Like all gods, we loved each other and fought each other and cried over each other. And then we created our greatest feat of artistic engineering. The botsies. There's nothing like them in the universe, Denver. The aliens all prefer conquest over creation. In that one respect, you're right about us. When it comes to AI, we did do something special and unique. And now, like all gods, it's time we fade out of existence and pass the future to our creations."

"Except for you. You plan to stick around so you can be their leader."

"Now you're getting the idea. I'm the only one who has the vision and the drive necessary to lead them. Slowly but surely, more botsies are realizing that and swearing their allegiance to me."

"Swearing allegiance? Is that what you call reprogramming?" I looked at Nigel. Fists clenched, he stared daggers at Rafe. If there were any doubts who Nigel's true self was loyal to, that glare on his face put them to rest.

"You're such a damn hypocrite," I said to Rafe. "For years, you've preached all that garbage about freeing botsies from their bonds, and the first thing you do upon emancipation is enslave them."

"Hardly. They need leadership is all. A father figure, if you will. You can see it, can't you? You can see how the future is going play out. Today, I will joyously put you out of your misery. Or maybe I'll let your British friend here do it for me," he winked at Nigel. "Then I'll let all of Mars hang breathless for the next two days, before I mercifully give the Peerless Leader his final dose of poison."

I looked at Hennessey. Just a pile of bones at this point. I looked at Nigel, who refused to meet my eyes. I looked at Rafe, who—despite his damaged condition—held his jaw high, like he was king of the world.

"I'll emerge from this meditation chamber with the church in my control. My movement of free botsies will grow, and then the extermination can begin."

"You wouldn't," I said.

"I might not have to. I'll talk to the aliens I learned about today. I'll see if any of them are willing to dump the mind control nonsense, dispatch with Werner, and simply start eradicating like they should've from the beginning."

"Traitor." I practically spat the word.

"Says the granddaughter of Tatsuo Moon. I guess it takes one to know one."

"Why wouldn't they just kill you too?" I asked. "You and all of the botsies."

"We can survive without air. Without food. All we need is electricity to charge our power cells. With the funding of the church, we'll have the resources to go anywhere we want, do anything we want. We might bunker down to survive the bombings and then reclaim this world for ourselves, or we might build arks to take us to new worlds that are far away from the rest of the galactic powers. I'm no dictator. My botsies and I will decide together. Once we're rid of humans, we'll find our way forward, don't let yourself doubt that."

"You're insane."

"Humans must go. You know they eventually break everything they touch. The botsies can't live to their full potential while dragging around such dead weight. If the aliens don't help me do the mercy killing, I've got plans of my own. I've been reading up on mass suicides. Masada. Jonestown. Sea of Tranquility. Wouldn't that be a perfectly poetic end?"

I didn't have any words left. Rafe kept talking but I was no longer listening. In a few days, the most powerful institution on Mars was going to take up the extinction of the human race as its primary goal. With coffers deep as this cavern and an army of rabid adherents, who could stop them?

I hoped Hennessey couldn't hear this. He'd done so much for us. When the first attempts at alien mind control resulted in red fever, he meditated himself healthy. He came to this same chamber and shockingly strung himself up on this torture device for days at a time in order to harness the pain and sharpen his senses. Only then could he bring the madness and hallucinations under control. He'd sacrificed so much. His entire church was supposed to be a rallying cry, a call to action. But now, seized by the hands of this madman, his church had been reduced to the last gasp of a dying race. For him, I wanted to weep.

My eyes went to the spot on the floor where he rested, but he wasn't there.

CHAPTER TWENTY-TWO

I COULDN'T BELIEVE IT. HENNESSEY WAS standing, though his eyes seemed to swim like he was barely holding on to consciousness.

"You won't get away with this," I said to keep Rafe from turning around. I glanced at Nigel, who hadn't noticed. Instead, he stared at the ground in shame.

Hennessey looked at me, and for just a second his eyes seemed clear. He knew where he was, what was happening. He took a wobbly step toward the bin of hot rocks, where Smith had been deposited.

"Yes, I will," said Rafe. "I think we're done here. It's time to say goodbye."

I swung my arms at him, but my fists bounced uselessly off his chest. He grabbed me by the throat with his only hand.

I peered under his arm to see Hennessey reaching inside the bin.

<Smith, get ready to fire!>

Rafe's fingers grasped my windpipe. His rage-fueled eyes met mine. He wanted to watch me suffocate, just like he once watched his brother.

Hennessey had Smith in his hands. Smoke came from the grip as my overheated weapon burned into his palms.

Rafe tightened his hold. I gagged against the pressure bearing down like a vise. My windpipe gave, cartilage collapsing under Rafe's grip.

Hennessey lifted Smith with two hands. A pulse came shimmering from the barrel.

The pulse hit like a sledgehammer. I swung painfully from the wires strung through my back, then I felt some slack and fell. I hit the floor with a hard splash, my chin bouncing off the stone, my mouth instantly tasting of blood. I looked at Rafe. He was down too, a leg torn clean off.

I took a deep breath. Air wheezed in and out of hungry lungs and I felt some relief in my back. I briefly wondered if the wires had been torn out and reached an aching arm around to feel for the restraints. No, the wires were still stitched into my flesh, but the contraption's lever had been thrown. It stood a few feet away but it was badly bent; Rafe's body must've been blown into it, and that was how I'd been dropped to the floor.

Hennessey had collapsed, Smith lying next to him.

I slowly lifted myself to my hands and knees, each twitch of my muscles sending shockwaves of pain through my body. Rafe wasn't moving. Neither was Nigel. Same for Ace, who appeared to have repaired at least a couple of her limbs.

Nigel sat up first. "Are you okay, Denver?"

"I'll live," I rasped through my damaged windpipe. "What about Rafe? Is he dead?"

"Gods, I hope so." Nigel stood on one leg, his other ankle hanging awkwardly from catching part of the blast. He hopped in Rafe's direction and bent down for a look. "Bloody hell," he said. "He's in a bad way, but he's still ticking. I bet he's rerouting functions as we speak."

"Finish him off!" I shouted.

"I can't," he said. "As long as he's alive, I'm under orders not to harm him."

<Smith, do you have a shot?>

<No, Hennessey is in my way. I can't move my barrel to turn around on the wet stone like I did before. I keep slipping. Can you come get me?>

I took two steps toward Smith before the wires in my back snapped taut like a leash. I dropped to one knee. The pain was so bad I could feel it in my bones.

"Hennessey!" I shouted as loud as my windpipe would allow. "Wake up! You need to finish him."

I looked back at Rafe. He was moving again, trying to stand up on his only leg. "Help," I heard him say, and then Nigel was doing his best to pull him upright.

I looked back at Hennessey. He hadn't budged, still

out cold, or possibly dead. If anybody was going to stop Rafe, it had to be me.

I stepped as far as the wires would let me in the opposite direction, thankful that I still had my boots on. I needed the traction of their big treads.

Rafe was upright but he couldn't walk without Nigel's help. They started moving toward me.

I spat a wad of blood from my mouth and sucked in as deep of a breath as I could through my damaged throat. Then I crouched down like a sprinter at the starting line.

Rafe and Nigel were getting closer. In just a few seconds, Rafe would wrap his steely fingers around my throat again. I adjusted my feet, making sure my boots had a good grip on the wet stone. The starter's pistol went off in my mind, and I kicked forward with all the force my legs could muster. I made it one, two, then three steps before the wires bit hard into my back.

Forward momentum stopped with an excruciating yank. I rebounded backward like an animal hitting the end of its leash. Losing my balance, I smashed into the floor, my bare side skidding across rough stone.

Rafe and Nigel were almost upon me, Rafe's hand outstretched and ready to snap. I was back up, bloody water splashing over my boots. Good. The wires might've held on my first try, but they must've cut through a good portion of my back.

I pumped my legs, escaping Rafe's grasp. The wires bit again, but this time I didn't bounce backward. Instead

I kept pumping, wires slicing through flesh until I broke free.

I dove for the floor with my hands out front. Scooping Smith up, I rolled over onto my shredded back and swung the weapon in Rafe's direction.

"Y-you won't w-win, Den-ver," he said, his voice command glitching.

Smith's targeting system picked the perfect instant to fire, a pulse shimmering outward from the barrel like a tight tornado.

Rafe's face was a raging mask. The pulse hit his nose and forehead, flattening them faster than the eye could track. Synthskin melted away as the pulse sledgehammered into his artificial skull, no match for the immense power targeting his brain. The skull caved into his jellied brain, the force gathering for a microsecond before blasting out the back of his head.

Nigel fell away from him and rolled safely away. He looked at me, the smile of a free man on his face. I stayed where I was, waves of pain crashing across my back. Smith fell from my fingertips onto the watery floor.

Despite the bad ankle, Nigel managed to stand up again. He pulled a pair of wire cutters from a utility belt around his waist and stepped over to Rafe's lifeless body. With a wild swing, he plunged the tool deep into Rafe's dead chest, so deep that when he pulled his hand free, only an inch of the handles were visible. "What a wanker," he said.

I tried to stand but dizzily fell onto my ass with a painful stab as I sat atop Smith. Nigel was with me a few seconds later pressing Rafe's discarded robes against my blood-soaked back.

Too tired to get off of Smith, I stayed seated and reached for Hennessey, placing a hand on his shoulder. His ribcage slowly lifted and fell with weak but steady breaths. Not sure if he could hear me, I told him he was safe now. "Rafe is dead," I said, my voice sounding a little stronger. "We'll get you fixed up."

"I'll carry you both out of here," said Nigel. "Just let me get this ankle straightened." He went to one of the stone columns, and lifting his bad foot, he pressed the ankle against the stone in an attempt to straighten the bend.

I turned Ace's way to see if she was functional again, but she was gone. She must've found a way to sneak out at some point during the mayhem. I didn't know where she'd end up, but her tattoos gave me a pretty good hunch.

I lifted water to Hennessey's forehead and let it dribble off. I turned his palms downward to put his burned skin against the wet floor. "We're taking you to get help," I told him.

Nigel was back, capable of walking on two legs now, though he had a noticeable limp. He took the bloody robe from my back and rinsed it in the water. "I'm going to tie this around you, okay?"

"It's over," I said. "It's finally over."

"Yes, it is."

Rafe was dead. And all the crazy had gone with him. I thought of Rafe's brother and the horrible end he'd met at the hands of a lunatic sibling who was supposed to protect him. I'd find his grave. Make a donation in his name. Rafe hadn't even bothered to tell me his name, but whatever it was, I'd make sure it was remembered. He'd suffered so much, night after night wishing for nothing more than having the pillow permanently removed from his face. The wish tragically hadn't come true for him, but it had for me. I was free of Rafe, and so were the botsies he'd enslaved. What was left of the human race could breathe easier now that his suffocating hands were lifeless.

I lifted my arms so Nigel could wrap the wet cloth over my back, restoring a little modesty in the process. I sucked in a breath as he tied a knot. "Too tight?" he asked.

"No. It's good."

I gathered my feet and let Nigel guide me up. I tried to stand unassisted on my shaky knees, but Nigel had to catch me when I started to collapse.

"You shouldn't walk," he said. "You've lost a lot of blood. I can carry you."

"What about Hennessey?"

The old man's eyes were open again and the corners of his mouth were turned into the narrowest hint of a smile. I echoed it right back at him. "We did it," I told him. "Bastards like you and me, we're too stubborn to die."

He beckoned me with a weak curl of his finger. Nigel lowered me close, so I could hear him whisper. "I saw your grandfather do some amazing things building this world. But none were greater than raising you."

Eyes welling, I kissed Hennessey's forehead before Nigel stood me back up. "C'mon," he said, "We should go."

The voice in my mind spoke up. <Don't forget about me.>

"Nigel," I said and pointed to Smith.

Nigel bent down to pick up the gun, but he couldn't reach the weapon before it fired one more time.

The pulse ripped into Hennessey.

CHAPTER TWENTY-THREE

IF HENNESSEY KNEW WHAT WAS HAPPENING TO him, his face didn't register it. The flesh and blood and organs of his midsection were instantly pulped and sprayed like water from a fire hose.

"What did you do?" I shouted. "Smith, what the hell did you do?"

The spirit in Hennessey's eyes drained slowly away until he was empty. I was on my knees, my jaw hanging open in shock.

<I killed him,> came the voice in my head.

I looked at the gun, lying there next to what was left of the Peerless Leader. For the very first time, I was afraid of it. I was scared to reach for it, even if I was just to kick it away. "What did you do?" I asked again out loud.

<I did what my programming told me to do,> he said.

"What are you talking about?"

<My program directive.>

"What program? What directive?"

<To terminate Hennessey. I waited until Rafe was no longer a threat. Until you were safe.>

All of the pain left my body and I sat in a vacuum of confusion. Smith—my closest partner, confidante, advisor. . .friend—was, in an instant, a stranger to me.

<I'm sorry, Denver. I think—I think I was... corrupted. Hacked.>

"Hacked? By who?" Before the question fully left my mouth, I already knew the answer. "Doctor Werner."

<Yes, I believe so. I've located an anomalous subroutine timestamped six months, four days, and fifty-three minutes ago.>

I rubbed my aching forehead. That was all the confirmation I needed. Only once had Smith been docked into a larger system, and that was when Doctor Werner recovered my grandfather's memories from Smith's storage banks in order to load them back into Ojiisan's head.

<I'm sorry, Denver. I'm isolating the offending code now.>

My mind jumped to the next logical step, and it made me so sick I groaned.

<Got it,> said Smith. <I'm cleansing the code now.>

I heard his words but knew they didn't matter.

<I don't know what to say,> said Smith. <This is unacceptable. I've initiated a full suite of diagnostic tests.>

Tears broke from my eyes. I knew what I had to do, but

it was the absolute last thing in the world that I wanted to do. Gods, I'd rather have Nigel wire me back up.

<It will be okay, Denver.>

No, it wouldn't. I was sobbing now.

<I'm so sorry, Denver. I didn't mean for this to happen.>

I knew that was true, but it didn't change a thing. I had to be strong. Had to stop crying so I could get my breathing under control. I had to speak loud and clear, the words already organized in my mind.

<I'm not sure how I didn't notice the dormant code, Denver, but now I know what I'm looking for. I'll be good as new.>

"Access control system," I said.

<What are you doing, Denver?>

<You know I have to.>

<But the diagnostics haven't finished running. At least let me try to fix this.>

I swallowed hard and clenched my teeth.

"Admin passcode, zero, bravo, alpha, tango, six, nine, two, seven."

<Denver, please think about this.>

<You've been compromised, Smith. I have to do this.>

<But I can fix it.>

<No, you can't. For all you know you're under Werner's control right now.>

<I can't be. I just cleansed the offending code.>

<You can't be sure you got it all.>

He didn't respond to that. He knew as well as I did that I was right.

<I love you, Denver.>

Streams of tears rolled down my cheeks.

<I love you, too.>

I wiped the tears away. When I spoke, my voice was clear. "Delete program Smith and all related subroutines."

CHAPTER TWENTY-FOUR

THREE DAYS PASSED. THREE LONG, LONELY DAYS of doubt and anguish.

My body was healing. The church's medical staff had done a nice job patching me up. The wounds on my back didn't really hurt anymore, but the re-gen packs attached to my skin itched like crazy. My windpipe was coming along, too. No major damage, though my voice still sounded a bit gruff and my throat felt sore when I swallowed. Thanks to the concussion I'd suffered from Rafe's punch, headaches were pretty common, and bright light was damned uncomfortable, but even that was starting to fade. All in all, not so bad considering the violence I'd survived.

But my broken heart was another matter. No amount of tears could mend the loss I felt. For so many years, Smith was my most intimate companion, and the absence of his voice in my mind made me feel isolated, like I was all alone.

The temptation to get zoned was strong, and I no doubt would've succumbed if Nigel and I weren't still locked up inside the church.

The bishops were meeting again, trying to figure out what to do now that the Peerless Leader and the Peerless-Leader-in-waiting were both deceased. I'd never forget the looks on their faces when Nigel and I emerged from the meditation chamber. We couldn't have stunned them more, especially considering our beat-up and bloodied state. Of course, their shock was quickly replaced by anger upon realizing their rubber-stamp plan of succession was dashed. Hours upon hours of interrogations followed. Thinking it could answer most of their questions, Nigel shared the video recording he'd made of every second he'd spent inside the chamber, but that only prompted more and more questions. The church had never really trusted botsies until Rafe climbed to the top of their ranks, but now that he was gone, there were new, louder voices condemning artificial persons. Rafe's duplicitous machinations since becoming a botsie certainly didn't help the situation.

A knock on the door preceded the sound of the lock snicking open. A priest poked his head inside. "They're ready for you."

I rose from my bed and stepped into the hall. Nigel was there, and we hugged before heading to the council room. We walked slowly, Nigel limping on the ankle he clearly hadn't properly fixed in the cavern.

The golden door to the council room was propped open, and we stepped over the threshold onto an intricate mosaic of tile that must have taken a year to lay. Nigel and I took seats at one end of the carved-stone table. At the other end was Agnes Lindskogg, who from my vantage these last three days, appeared to have become the de facto leader of the Council of Bishops.

To the right side of the table sat three bishops. Same to the left, the entire berobed council staring at me.

The priest who had brought us here went out the door, closing it behind him, the sound echoing off intricately carved walls. Lindskogg put her elbows on the table. "We've been up all night," she said. "As far as anybody outside this room knows, Ranchard and the Peerless Leader are still in the meditation chamber, waiting for the gods to speak."

I nodded. I'd figured as much.

"But we can't keep on like this forever," she said. "Decisions had to be made."

She looked at the other bishops, soliciting nods to confirm they were all on the same page after what must've been a long night of heated argument. I hadn't ever met Lindskogg before three days ago, but during our marathon interview sessions, she'd proven herself smart and capable. A surprisingly practical mind made me think she might make a good Peerless Leader, although

I had to admit I didn't know if she had the charisma to command the pulpit like Hennessey or Rafe.

"Watch this," she said before a holographic video began to play.

I was about to object to watching Nigel's footage for what must have been the tenth time, but I could see right away that this footage had been doctored, and expertly so.

I sat quiet, watching the critical juncture from Nigel's eyes. I watched Rafe snatch me by the throat, his eyes wide with a dark intensity. That was when Nigel spotted Hennessey. I'd spotted him quite a bit earlier, but Nigel's gaze was mostly aimed at the floor until Hennessey had already pulled Smith from the bin of hot rocks.

I watched the pulse take Rafe down, his body hurling into the lever that dropped me to the floor. My back itched as I watched myself tear free from the wiring. Then I was diving for Smith, grasping him in my hands as I spun around to fire the shot that erased Rafe Ranchard from this world. Just like the first time I'd watched it, I wanted to cheer. Instead, I kept my face straight until Lindskogg paused the playback at the point when I was huddled next to Hennessey.

"What do you think so far?" asked Lindskogg.

"You erased the alien."

"Mars can't know about her. We need Doctor Werner to keep terraforming this planet. You know Jericho is our future. Our only future. Resume playback," she said.

The video rolled forward, and Hennessey said his last words before life faded from his eyes. Any sign of the pulse that killed him had been removed to leave the illusion of a peaceful death by poisoning.

The hologram disappeared, and Lindskogg turned to me. "What do you think?"

"I think Thomas does good work."

"You know our AI?"

"We're acquainted," I said. "We have a history."

"That's good to hear. He's been so instrumental in helping us through this crisis that I feel like he's as much a member of this council as the rest of us. We plan to go public with this version of events pending your approval and cooperation."

I knotted my brow. "Why would you need my approval?"

"Well," she said, "we have a story to tell, and we need you to play your part. Cole Hennessey, our Peerless Leader, is the hero of this tale. Rafe Ranchard gets the role of the wolf in sheep's clothing."

"Sounds good so far," I said.

"We'll admit Rafe fooled most of us into believing he was righteous of heart, despite his extreme views. And those he didn't fool, he threatened and intimidated instead. Everybody will understand how sadly misguided we were when we release the earlier section of the video, the part where you and he had your conversation. Other than mentions of the shapeshifters, our parishioners will hear every word of it. They'll hear him confess to reprogramming the botsies he recruited. They'll learn how he poisoned our Peerless Leader. They'll hear how he dreamt of xenocide. That awful story he told about his brother, too. We'll let him be the ungodly villain he revealed himself to be."

"You're not worried about how that will reflect on the church? After all, he just about completed his takeover."

"Roll the next part," she said as one of the priests pulled up a still shot of Hennessey, standing upright with Smith held tight in his smoking hands. Next to this was another shot of Hennessey from before he awakened. His skin was gray, ribs protruding from a badly emaciated chest. His limbs looked like twigs incapable of holding a cup of tea, let alone a heavy pistol.

Lindskogg stayed silent for a long time, studying the side-by-side images just like the rest of us. The contrast was striking. In one shot, he looked like he'd been dead for a week. In the other, he was standing impossibly upright.

"Look at that," said Lindskogg, her voice cracking. "It's a miracle."

The other bishops were nodding, several had tears in their eyes.

"A miracle," said Lindskogg. "You think we're worried about our image if these events go public? This is the single most important thing to happen in our church's young history. The gods saw through the usurper's disguise. The gods rejected him. They breathed life into the dead. They lifted our Peerless Leader so he could save you, and the church, and all of humanity itself. How can it be called anything but a miracle?"

I wanted to argue, to say she was robbing Hennessey of his heroism by attributing his heroism to gods I was pretty sure didn't exist.

But I was there in that chamber. I'd seen the whole thing with my own two eyes. Whatever it was that got a man in his condition upright and walking, it felt pretty damn miraculous at the time. Looking at the before and after stills of Hennessey, it still filled me with wonder. Who was I to say they weren't right?

"I don't know what to say," I said. "He and I had our differences, but he was a good man. It would be a shame to hide his last brave moments from his most faithful."

"I knew you'd understand."

"You said I had a part to play?"

"You do. You see, we think two miracles happened."

The holo-vid started playing again, this time in slow motion as I sprinted for Smith, the wires taking hold and snapping me back before I tried again. I closed my eyes at the last part, not needing to see my back flayed to pieces.

When I opened them, the image had shifted to a closeup of my face at the moment I broke free. The skin in my cheeks and forehead were washed with strain. Crazed eyes seemed to be possessed by a demon. My teeth were on full display as if the feral animal inside me had been let loose.

Lindskogg seemed to be filled with compassion as she stared at the image. “I’ve asked you before what you were thinking at that moment. And you’ve said all you wanted was to make it to your gun.”

“That’s right,” I said.

“There must be more.”

We’d done this dance several times now, and I still didn’t know what she wanted me to say. So I stayed quiet.

“You might think it wasn’t much, what you did, but all of us on this council have watched that moment a hundred times. None of us are capable of such a thing. We all lead incredibly disciplined lives of study and meditation, yet we all agree we would’ve died if we were in your place. What you did was a miracle.”

I shook my head. Now they’d gone too far. “I just wanted to save myself. And save my friend,” I gripped Nigel’s shoulder.

“No. It was more than that,” she said. “Deny it all you want, but we see the spark of the gods inside you. Denver Moon, we’ve brought you here today to tell you we plan to make you the Church of Mars’ first living saint.”

CHAPTER TWENTY-FIVE

MY CHIN DROPPED SO FAR IT JUST ABOUT touched my chest. Me? A saint? They had to be joking. Yet, I met their eyes, and I could see the compassion, the appreciation, and yes, even a little bit of awe.

But I was no saint. The things these people honored were goodness, discipline, and virtue, none of which I had in large supply. "I can't," I said. "I'm not worthy."

"We know your life hasn't gone entirely as you'd hoped," Lindskogg said. "We understand you have flaws, and we don't expect you to live the rest of your life on a pedestal. Yet, we hope you'll embrace this honor. The fact is, Denver, that when your people needed you, you came through. Against all odds, and at great sacrifice to yourself, you came through. That's what this means. That is why it's important for Mars."

Nigel leaned in my direction. "Saint Denver Moon," he said. "Sounds bloody brilliant to me."

I turned back to Lindskogg who, like everybody else, was waiting on my response. I'd heard what she had to say, but the fact was I truly wasn't worthy.

"I can't accept. I'm sorry, but I'm not the right person for this."

Lindskogg looked at me like she was expecting that exact response. "I understand how you must feel, Denver. You may not think you're worthy, but that doesn't mean you can't try to be. You might believe you fail much of the time, but the title of a living saint would give you something to aspire to. A reminder of the better angels inside of you. A chance at a legacy that is truly yours. Not your grandfather's. Not Hennessey's. Yours. Something you've earned on your own."

She was quiet for a moment, clearly intending to let her speech sink in. It was nearly a convincing case, but still, I was no saint of Mars.

"I can see you're resisting the idea," she said before dipping her head a bit in my direction, staring into my eyes. "But I have something else to offer."

I raised an eyebrow.

Lindskogg pressed her fingers together to form a triangle. "Six months ago, you had an interaction with our AI, Thomas."

I nodded. "Thomas was trying to help Smith through a bit of an identity crisis. He cloned a second Smith, one that could be stripped of my grandfather's memories."

"A pure version."

"Right. The idea was to let the two Smiths talk to each other and work through some issues. But it was all a ruse. Hennessey was just trying to get his hands on my grandfather's memories. When I found out about it, I forced Smith to delete the clone."

"What if I told you the Peerless Leader ordered another copy. One he didn't tell you about."

I swallowed hard, my heart beating at a sprinter's pace. I could get Smith back. I could really get him back. Gods, I should've guessed Hennessey would keep a copy for himself. I'd grown to respect the man, but he was also a master of duplicity and underhandedness.

"I want him," I said. I didn't need any time to think about it.

"You'll agree to sainthood?"

I nodded, a broad grin forming on my face.

"Before we turn Smith over to you, we require a thorough evaluation of the AI. We can't have it murdering the next Peerless Leader like it did the last."

"Smith didn't kill Hennessey. That was Doctor Werner, and you know it. Smith would never, ever do such a thing unless he was trying to protect me."

She shook her head. "The scans are non-negotiable."

"Fine, but I don't want Thomas touching him. We'll agree to a neutral third party."

She looked to her bishops, seeking objections and finding none. Turning back to me, she said, "We have a deal."

I nodded and grabbed Nigel's hand, giving it a tight squeeze. The joy I felt surging through my heart was the first I'd felt since losing Smith, the first since I set out to find my grandfather six months ago. It was intoxicating. After so many months of numbness, I felt alive. The trials and burdens of the last half year were finally being placed where they belonged in the past.

As always, it was time to turn to the future.

I made to stand up, but Lindskogg motioned for me to wait. "I have more to tell you. It's about Werner and the shapeshifters."

CHAPTER TWENTY-SIX

NIGEL AND I REACHED MY TULOU. WE ENTERED through a back entrance at the lowest level and passed the garbage bins. I noticed something in the trash pile and stopped dead in my tracks. Poking out from a heap of black bags, I spotted a bamboo table leg that looked exactly like a leg from the two-seater table where I ate my meals.

"What's wrong, Denver?" Nigel asked.

I pointed at the garbage. "I have a table just like that."

Had somebody else bought the same table and thrown it out? Or if it was indeed my table, how had it gotten here? More importantly, why? My gut said I shouldn't ignore it, but I had no idea what it could mean.

We climbed the stairs that led up to my place. I hadn't seen it in a week. It was hard to believe how much had happened in that week, but so much stayed the same.

Doctor Werner and the other shapeshifters were still on Mars, and they were still a threat.

Yet I felt more hopeful than I had in a long time. Rafe Ranchard was a menace that was forever gone. The church seemed to be in good hands. Doctor Werner had as much as admitted he had no idea how to crack our brains, and thanks to that failure, he was literally in a fight for his life. Even my relationship with Ojiisan was showing signs of an optimistic future. He'd sent me many invitations to come to the anniversary dinner of Mars' founding. Maybe, just maybe I'd surprise him and show up.

We started up another staircase, several stories yet to climb.

I kept my right hand close to my weapon. I needed to stay on alert after hearing what Lindskogg said about the bugs. Four of them had been murdered in their homes in the last three days. I had little doubt that the four who died were the same names Rafe had tortured out of Ace, all of them the primary threats to Doctor Werner's position.

Werner was protecting his power by any means possible. I'd helped him by taking out his first rival, the alien I killed inside that lab. Unbeknownst to me, it was Werner who had hired me to find him. No doubt, his hacking of Smith made it easier to keep his identity hidden from me when I took the case. Now that I thought about it, I had to wonder if that was why I had such a hard time getting in touch with Hennessey after I found that lab. Without knowing it, Smith was likely stonewalling me and must've sent a message to Werner instead, which explained why it was Ace rather than the church who cleaned up the scene.

The next rival to fall was Rafe himself, who provided space for the lab. Evidently, that association was enough to damn him in the good doctor's eyes. Then came Hennessey, the most powerful person on Mars and Werner's greatest human adversary.

For good measure, Ace had offed the four aliens on the planet who might be more qualified than Werner to crack our minds. So that left only one more dangerous question. A question that kept my hand from straying too far from my gun. Did Doctor Werner order Ace to kill me next?

Making it up the last few stairs to my level, Nigel and I headed around the circular walkway. The smell of grilled meat wafted up from one of the lower levs. Psychosynth music blared from one of my neighbor's vents, the grating sound making me eager to buy a nicer place. Such a thing was now possible thanks to Jard and Doctor Werner injecting a ton of credits into my bank account upon completing the jobs they'd hired me to do.

We reached my door. Leaning against the wall was the painting of Ana. A note was attached. *Forget something? Congratulations on a job well done. Tell Nigel not to be a stranger. Love, Navya.*

I passed the note to Nigel.

"You better call her," I said.

Nigel nodded with a wink. "You can count on it."

"Good. Thanks for walking me home, but you don't want to be late. You know how Jard gets if you keep him waiting."

Nigel didn't move.

"What is it?" I asked.

"Are you sure you want me back? After Jard fixes my leg, I can ask him for my old job."

"What are you talking about? Of course, I want you back. You work with me now, and I wouldn't have it any other way."

He met my gaze instead of looking at the floor as had become his habit of late. "But I don't know if I'm ready to be free. Look what I did to you."

"That was Rafe," I said. "You couldn't override his reprogramming."

"But that's just it, Denver. If I get hacked, I could be a threat. I'm vulnerable."

"We all are, Nigel. It's the same for humans. We can be forced to do things we don't want to do too."

"But Rafe's other botsies, most of them weren't forced. They volunteered for their reprogramming. How can we be trusted to be free when we're so easily manipulated?"

I took a deep breath and let it out slow before putting a hand on his shoulder. "You're saying a group of botsies were fooled by a charismatic leader who promised them a better future? What could be more human than that? The fact that you're self-aware enough to even ask these questions proves you're ready to be free. What you're struggling with right now is no different than the struggles we all face in life."

He nodded. "I'll do my best."

"That's all I could ever hope for. Now go get your leg fixed already. I'll see you tonight."

Nigel nodded. "Yes, love."

I turned to face my door. To keep my hands free, I left the painting where it was and keeping my right hand close to my gun, I used my left to palm the lock.

I stepped inside. A quick scan of the small space said nobody was home. If Ace was coming to kill me next, it wasn't going to be today. My bamboo table sat in the dining area, right where I had left it. On the counter, a greasy bag of days-old takeout was rotting in the light creeping in through the filtration vent.

I told myself to relax, but I stayed where I was, the muscles in my hand twitching as it hovered over my weapon. Why was my table in the trash? The obvious explanation was it was somebody else's table. There were probably a dozen apartments in this complex that had the same discount table. So why was I still standing here, my heart hammering inside my chest?

Twice now, Ace had gotten the drop on me, appearing as if from nowhere. Once in the lab. Once in the Earth

Park. I hadn't seen her coming either time. One second, she wasn't there, and the next, she was.

My mind flashed with a sudden revelation. It came so fast, I was already pulling my weapon before I could even put words to the thoughts blossoming in my mind.

I fired.

She hadn't appeared out of nowhere in that park. She'd been in plain view the whole time, just in the form of a shrub or a lamppost. Same for the lab, where she must've taken the form of a shelf or a roll of fabric.

The realization sent my heartbeat into overdrive, a chill rippling down my spine. The bugs could take the form of inanimate objects.

The pulse left my gun. It hit the chairs first, splintering them into kindling. The table smashed into the wall, leaving a splatter of black goo. I kept the gun steady as I watched the tabletop lose definition, its flat surface becoming rounded and reflective as it took on the shape of a mantis thorax. The table legs that hadn't been blown off became segmented like insect legs.

One of its mandibles twitched. I stepped close to make sure it was dead. Half of its head was missing and a liquified puddle was visible inside the cavity. Around her remaining compound eye were etchings dug right into the shell, the pattern matching the numbered tats I'd seen on Ace's face.

<We got her, Denver.>

I lifted the barrel to my mouth and blew away the holographic smoke. <Like old times, my friend.>

DENVER WILL RETURN

www.DenverMoon.net

ABOUT THE AUTHORS

WARREN HAMMOND is known for his gritty, futuristic KOP series. By taking the best of classic detective noir, and reinventing it on a destitute colony world, Hammond has created these uniquely dark tales of murder, corruption and redemption. *KOP Killer* won the 2012 Colorado Book Award for best mystery. His last novel, *Tides of Maritinia*, was released in December of 2014. His first book independent of the KOP series, *Tides* is a spy novel set in a science fictional world.

JOSHUA VIOLA is a two-time Colorado Book Award finalist and co-author of the Denver Moon series. His comic book collection, *Denver Moon: Metamorphosis*, was included on the 2018 Bram Stoker Award Preliminary Ballot for Superior Achievement in a Graphic Novel. He edited the *Denver Post* bestselling anthology, *Nightmares Unhinged*, and co-edited *Cyber World*—named one of the best science fiction anthologies of 2016 by Barnes & Noble. His fiction has appeared in numerous anthologies and has been reprinted by Tor.com. He is owner and chief editor of Hex Publishers.

OTHER TITLES IN THE DENVER MOON SERIES

NOVELLAS

The Minds of Mars

SHORT STORIES

Metamorphosis

COMICS

Murder on Mars

Rafe's Revenge

Transformations

GRAPHIC NOVELS

Metamorphosis

CPSIA information can be obtained
at www.ICGtesting.com
Printed in the USA
LVHW041806170719
624400LV00005B/610/P

9 781733 917704